CLOUDS

CLOUDS

IRON HORSE MYSTERY #4

C.J. SHANE

Published by Rope's End Publishing

ISBN 978-1-951524-30-2

Typesetting services by BOOKOW.COM

Acknowledgments

Sincere thanks go to Tucson graphic designer Lynne East-Itkin for the book cover design, and to Dawn Lewis of County Durham, England, for editorial services. And thanks to my beta readers, too.

Letty Valdez Mysteries

Desert Jade 2017
Dragon's Revenge 2018
Daemon Waters 2019
Direct Evidence 2022

Cat Miranda Mysteries

Kissed 2020
Fair Play 2021
The Broken Pot 2022

Iron Horse Mysteries

Take Four #1 2023
Shadow Man #2 2023
In the Slips #3 2024
Clouds #4 2024
A Closer Look #5 2024

CONTENTS

1. Sunday Potluck

David Li Liang checked the boiling pot on his stove then glanced at the stove's clock. Three more minutes. He sighed and went to sit on his sofa. Bonita, the almost-grown kitten, or maybe she should be called a cat now, came to sit on his lap. He began to stroke her, and Bonita purred contentedly.

"You're kinda spoiled, you know?" Li said. Bonita looked up at him with her big golden eyes and purred even louder. She was a tri-color calico cat, which, for Li, was the prettiest kitty in the world.

He sighed again. "Dumplings. I'm taking dumplings to the potluck again." That's what his fellow residents at Casa Pacifica Apartments called his *jiaozi* at their Sunday potluck dinners. Or worse, Italian "*ravioli*." He grimaced. As if the English or Italians were the first at making those delicious meat and veggie-filled, small dough bundles with their edges pressed together, and then boiled in hot water. Ridiculous! The Italians got their dumplings from China! The story was that Marco Polo brought *jiaozi* back to Italy when he returned from his travels. *Jiaozi*'s origin was China!

"So why can't they use the proper name?" he groused. Bonita purred even louder.

Li frowned. On top of that, his *jiaozi* had some excellent *jiangyou* sauce poured over them, too, sauce that came all the way from Zhejiang Province in China. Just as *jiaozi* became "dumplings" at the Sunday potlucks, the potluck gang transformed *jiangyou* into "soy sauce." Li just couldn't get it. Mandarin Chinese words were not *that* hard to say. They had no trouble saying Spanish or French words, but they wouldn't even try Mandarin.

Charlie was the exception. Logan Reid, Casa Pacifica's manager, had a five-year-old son named Charlie, and Charlie seemed to be the only one with an adventuresome spirit when it came to trying new words. Li had already taught Charlie how to say a couple of Mandarin phrases. He laughed to himself. Maybe he'd teach Charlie even more Mandarin, the two of them would have their own conversations, and the adults wouldn't understand a word.

Meanwhile, he had to make *jiaozi* way too often, always at their request. He was one of Tucson's top chefs, he knew how to make a long list of delicious Chinese dishes, but no. It had to be *jiaozi*. If they started pouring Italian or Mexican sauces on his *jiaozi*, he was going to quit, and start making tacos every Sunday! It would serve them right. He shook his head.

"Truth be told, I'm not really mad about the *jiaozi*," he muttered to Bonita. He knew what was making him so annoyed. It was his parents who were bothering the hell out of him. His parents and their "suggestion" that he get married, and worse, get married to a girl they had picked out for him. No way! *That* was what was bothering him. And if he admitted it to himself, he was getting a little tired of his chef job. His restaurant manager was a worry wart, stressed out all the time, and now the manager was putting pressure on everyone in the kitchen to work harder faster. Why not just chill out? On top of all that, Laurel was gone now so he didn't even have the relief of physical pleasure with her.

"Bonita, I'm very cranky. I need to get over myself before I go join the others." He looked at the clock. Time was up for the damn dumplings.

He pushed Bonita onto the sofa, went to the stove, turned it off, and drained the pot of all the hot water. Then he transferred the *jiaozi* to a large ceramic serving bowl. He added the *jiangyou* sauce.

Li carefully placed the very full and very hot ceramic bowl into his favorite carrying basket. Yes, the bowl was hot from freshly cooked *jiaozi*, but he was going immediately to Logan's apartment downstairs for the regular Sunday potluck. He would be able to get the bowl out of the basket and on a table trivet pretty quickly without burning himself or the basket.

Li glanced in the mirror on his way out. He didn't look too bad. His goatee and mustache were neatly trimmed, his long dark hair was tied back into a braid, and he was wearing a new shirt, sort of a pale blue color. He never wore white when he wasn't working. White was too much like the uniform he wore as a chef. Li closed his door behind him, making sure that Bonita the cat stayed inside his apartment and didn't go wandering. This was the time of evening that the coyotes came out, and they were looking for something good to eat, preferably a chubby little kitty.

Thinking about the potluck made Li wonder who would be there tonight. Okay, so apartment manager Logan and his boy Charlie would definitely be there, and Logan's girlfriend, Zoey, the biology teacher who lived downstairs in her own apartment. Marc and Angela would probably be there, too. Angela had just moved in with Marc, and they seemed very happy together. The two of them had a big dog named Gwenny. Bonita had not met Gwenny yet. Probably for the best. Gwenny seemed pretty tame, but she was a big dog, a greyhound. Bonita would be terrified.

Li's thoughts turned to the newest resident in their Casa Pacifica apartment building in the Iron Horse district of Tucson. Xochi. He'd first met her when she and Angela were assaulted by some dipwad who vandalized Angela's mobile veterinarian van, whacked both women in their faces, and then ran away. Her name was Xochi, obviously a Mexican name. Sounded like "SO-chee." She was very pretty, with a sort of feisty manner and a "don't mess with me" attitude. Her apartment was upstairs, too, down the hall from him, but he hadn't seen much of her, despite being really curious about her. He knew she was some kind of artist. She made artist's books, whatever that was. He thought artists painted or made sculptures, not books. Yes, he looked forward to knowing her better.

He knocked on Logan's door and then opened it.

"Hey, Li. Come on in," Logan called out. He was wearing a chef's apron and holding a large spoon in his hand. "I've made a veggie-chicken stew. It's almost ready."

Li approached the long dining table, pulled the ceramic bowl out of his basket and put it on a trivet. Li respected Logan a lot, and trusted him, too. Li had found Logan to be a fair and capable manager of the apartment building where they lived, and over time, he'd come to admire Logan, too. The man was a real intellectual who was finishing his doctoral degree in philosophy, of all things. Li could have been intimated because he didn't know beans about philosophy. But Logan was never arrogant, and Li had come to admire what a good job Logan did of fathering Charlie. He thought of Logan as a real friend.

"I brought some…," Li hesitated. "…dumplings." He looked into the living area and saw Marc, Angela, and the new resident, Xochi, sitting together. He waved, and they all said hello and waved back.

Just then, Charlie came running out of his bedroom with Gwenny the greyhound on his heels. "Dumplings!" he said in a loud voice. He stopped suddenly, and Gwenny ran into his backside. Charlie laughed loudly as the dog skidded into him. "No! I mean *jiaozi!*"

Li chuckled. "That's right. So Charlie, *'Ni jiào shénme míngzì?'*" What's your name?

Charlie giggled and started jumping up and down. *'Wo jiào cháli.'* My name is Charlie.

"Very good." Li was grinning now. They'd practiced this earlier. Now it was time to try something new. He pointed at Gwenny and asked, "*'Tā jiào shénme míngzì?'*" What's her name?

For a moment, Charlie looked blank, then he asked, "*'Tā'?*"

Li nodded. He put his hand on his chest and said, "*Wo,*" then pointed at Charlie and said, "*Ni,*" then pointed at Gwenny. "*Tā. Tā jiào shénme míngzì?*"

Charlie nodded and giggled, "*Tā jiào Gwenny.*" Her name is Gwenny.

"*Hao de, hao de.*" Very good. Li was grinning now. "Your colloquial Mandarin is very good."

"What's 'colloquial?'" Charlie looked confused.

"Common language. Words used most often."

Charlie turned and threw his arms around the greyhound who was wagging her tail. "I love you, Gwenny."

"*Wo ài ni.* That means 'I love you.'" Li said.

"*Wo ài ni,* Gwenny!" Charlie couldn't stop giggling. Gwenny's tail wagged faster.

Li glanced around. All the adults were grinning, too. Xochi smiled at him and said, "Impressive. You're a good language teacher."

Li suddenly felt embarrassed. He was acting like a show off. First cranky, and then a show off. What the hell is wrong with me? he asked himself. He looked up and saw both Logan and his girlfriend Zoey grinning proudly.

"I didn't know that you are teaching him Chinese," Zoey said.

"Yeah, Mandarin. Charlie is really sharp. He likes to learn new things."

Logan nodded. "Yes, I'm really proud of him." He stepped away from the table. "Charlie, go wash your hands and be quick about it. It's time to eat. Everyone come and have a seat at the table."

A few minutes later, they were all seated together for their Sunday potluck.

"Thank you all for coming," Logan said. "I made this stew, and Zoey grilled some salmon steaks."

"I made a creole rice and beans dish. It includes some smoked sausage," Angela added. "My mom used to make it, New Orleans style."

"I made nothing. I'm lazy," Marc added. Everyone chuckled.

"And I made dumplings again," Li shrugged his shoulders.

"Good thing. We'd have to protest if we don't get our dumplings," Logan nodded.

"*Jiaozi*, Daddy," Charlie said.

"Okay. *Jiaozi*," Logan replied.

Li smiled and nodded. Maybe Charlie would take care of the language problem for him.

Logan poured wine, passed the glasses around, and handed Charlie a glass of orange juice. They commenced eating. The meal went fast and, not long after, they were seated in a circle in Logan's living room.

"I'd like to know what everyone has been up to," Logan said. "I'll start. I'll begin teaching my Introduction to Philosophy class at Pima Community College this week. I'll have a second class in Social Philosophy the next day. And I'm working on an academic paper about human rights, specifically the right to privacy versus freedom of expression in the context of digital media."

"Wow! That's a mouthful," Marc said. Marc Tomassone had returned to Tucson only recently after long months away working as a photojournalist in war zones. He brought Gwenny the greyhound with him, very quickly met veterinarian Dr. Angela Brooks, they fell in love, and not long after, Angela became part of the Casa Pacifica family. Gwenny spent part of her time with Marc and Angela, and a good bit of time as well with Charlie. Gwenny and Charlie adored each other.

"Yeah," Logan chuckled. "Most people aren't interested in what I do unless it affects them directly. Then they suddenly discover that they have an opinion on the subject. In this case, folks seem to be interested in the topic." He took Zoey's hand in his. "Tell us what you're up to."

"Spring semester is finished. I'm going to teach a summer biology course at the high school, and I'm thinking about applying for a grant to start an ornithology program for five- and six-year-olds. We'll go birding a couple of times a week, always early in the day before it gets too hot."

"I'm going with her if that happens!" Charlie said enthusiastically. "And right now, I'm going to summer camp every day."

Logan shifted attention to Marc. "How about you?"

"Angela convinced me that I'm not half bad at photography. I mean art photography. So I've been wandering around Tucson and taking photos. I'm starting to enter my work into some local art exhibits." Angela took his hand and smiled. Marc added, "This is way more fun than taking photos of people shooting each other in war zones." He nodded to Angela.

"My boss gave me a pay raise at my job," Angela grinned. "And I'm spending more time in the clinic and less time in the mobile vet unit. My boss is definitely hiring two new vet assistants, and he may even hire a new veterinarian who will take over the mobile unit. We're really busy."

"Li? How's your chef job? And how's your friend Laurel?"

"Laurel and I parted company," Li said. "She was accepted into Princeton University's law school so she's moved back east to New Jersey. I could have gone with her, but I don't think I would be happy there. It's okay. She's doing what she wants, and so am I. We parted on good terms. No hard feelings." He shrugged his shoulders. "Not much else is new." He looked at Xochi. "Tell us about you." He didn't want to talk about any of the cranky stuff.

"Everything is going well. I turned my second bedroom into a studio, and I've already taught two book arts classes there. Photos of one of my artist's books will be included in an art book to be published soon. The book is devoted exclusively to artist's books so it's a real honor for me to be included. And…"

Suddenly there was a crashing sound that came from above them, then some thumping sounds.

Xochi jumped up. "That noise came from my apartment!" She moved quickly toward the door. "Someone is in my apartment!"

Li immediately followed her. "I'll go with you. If there's an intruder, he may try to confront you."

Logan and Marc were on their feet now, too. Logan turned to Charlie, "You stay here with Zoey."

Just as Xochi opened Logan's door, they all could hear the sound of someone running down the upstairs hallway in their apartment building. As they stepped into the hall, a form dressed in dark clothing and a black mask could be seen rushing down the stairs and exiting the building through the small laundry room and backdoor.

"I'll follow him!" Logan said. "He may go out back down the alley."

Marc was opening the front door at the same time. "I'll go out front in case he comes around and tries to run down the street."

By now, Xochi and Li were already upstairs at Xochi's apartment, which was directly above Logan's. Xochi reached out for the closed door, which opened easily. "Look! Someone must have picked the lock."

Li stepped forward. "Let me go in first. There may still be someone here." He entered the apartment ahead of her. He could feel Xochi close to him, her hand on his back. The apartment was silent.

Xochi moved forward and looked around Li. "I don't see anything disturbed. I'll look in my bedroom and studio." Li followed her. She glanced around the living room, then she went to her bedroom. "Looks okay," she said. Then she went to the extra bedroom that she had transformed into a studio and a room for small classes. Li came to her side. Xochi gasped.

The room was trashed. The only piece of furniture that had not been overturned was the large, heavy table in the middle of the room. There were three six- and eight-foot tall shelving units that had been overturned. Art supplies were everywhere. Li could see large cardboard folders full of art papers of various weights that were scattered across the floor. Also on the floor were jars of stencil paints and bottles of various colored inks, tubes of acrylic paint, and a couple of large plastic gallon containers full of some thick white liquid. The lid of one of the gallon containers had come off, and the white liquid had spilled onto numerous items.

Xochi reached over and sat the plastic gallon container upright. "Oh, god. What a mess! There's PVA glue all over the place. And my container of methyl cellulose powder is dumped out, too." She turned and opened the door to the room's closet. Same thing. The shelves were empty, and what had been on the shelves was now on the floor.

Li looked down at Xochi. He could see the tears in her eyes as she looked up at him.

"I don't understand. Who would do something like this? There's so much damage. It's going to cost me a lot to replace everything. And a lot of time to clean up this mess."

He put his arm around her shoulders. "I'll help you. What about your work? Your artist's books, I mean?"

"They're in containers in drawers in that big chest in the living room." She walked back into the living room. "Nothing disturbed there."

Logan and Marc appeared. Logan was shaking his head. "He got away. I didn't see him at all in the back."

"And he wasn't in the front either. I'm going to check the video surveillance camera we set up earlier," Marc added.

"Xochi, what about the lock on your door?" Logan asked.

Xochi took a look. "It must have been picked. I don't see any damage or signs that the door was forced."

"No one has a copy of your key?" Marc asked

"No." Xochi shook her head.

"What about previous tenants?" he asked Logan.

"I have the locks to individual apartments changed every time there's a change of residents. So it can't be that," Logan said. "Let's go down to my apartment. We can call the cops, and I want to check the front and back doors."

Ten minutes later they were all back in Logan's apartment. He looked and found that either the front door or the back door of the apartment building had been picked open. He decided it was the back door. No damage had been done, but the back door was unlocked. By that time, Marc had retrieved the video from the surveillance camera.

Marc gestured to the screen. "Here he is at the back door. He appears to be a man from his build, and he's fairly tall. He's dressed all in black. You can see him pull a tool out from his back pocket and start messing with the back door lock. It only takes him a minute to get the door open."

Logan shook his head. "I'll have to talk to the owners and get better locks."

There was a knock at Logan's door, and when he opened it, two Tucson police officers in uniform were standing there.

Logan introduced himself, explained the situation, and led them upstairs to Xochi's apartment. They all stood aside as she opened her door. The cops went in, examined the debris, took photos and notes, and asked a few questions. Logan noticed that they also dusted for fingerprints. They took Xochi's fingerprints, too, so they would know hers as well.

One of the cops with the name tag "Officer Morales" on his chest said, "Okay. We have the basic information and photos. One of our detectives will be around in the morning to ask more questions. Meanwhile, Ms. Navarro, I suggest you compile a list of missing and damaged or destroyed items. And since your building's outer doors and your apartment door are so easy to break into, perhaps you could spend the night in a safer place. The perpetrator might return."

Li frowned. He didn't like this at all. Neither did Logan or Marc who were both frowning, too.

The police officers left, and Logan turned to Xochi. "Do you have somewhere you can go?"

Xochi shook her head. "No, it's too late now to call any friends. I don't have any family here in Tucson." She shrugged her shoulders. "I'll just stay in my apartment. Whoever did this made a huge mess and caused a lot of damage. I seriously doubt that they will return."

The three men, Zoey, and Angela all shook their heads.

"How about if you sleep on our couch?" Logan asked her.

"Oh, I think you are all making too big a deal of this."

"Please reconsider, Xochi," Zoey said.

"Okay. That's it. I'm sleeping on your couch, or you're sleeping on my couch," Li said firmly.

Everyone nodded their approval. Everyone but Xochi. She giggled.

"What's so funny?" Li frowned. "Think I can't take care of you? I know a little *gong fu*."

"I don't know what's funny," she answered. Then Xochi burst into tears.

Zoey and Angela put their arms around her as she sobbed. "Listen to Li," Angela said. "He's trying to help you. He knows *gong fu*." She turned to Li and whispered, "What's *gong f* u?"

"Chinese martial arts," Li answered. "*Kung fu*, if you prefer." He was annoyed. Does Xochi think just because he's a chef, he doesn't know how to take care of a woman?

Xochi wiped away her tears and looked up at Li. "Thank you for the offer. May I please sleep on your couch tonight?"

"Yes, you may," he answered in a serious tone of voice. "Bring your favorite pillow." Li felt a sudden sense of elation. He wasn't sure why.

Logan spoke up. "Okay, it's getting late. It's way past Charlie's bedtime. Let's all settle down for the night. Li, I'll text you in the morning when the detective arrives, no doubt with a long list of questions. We'll get the investigation going. We need to find out who did this and why, so it doesn't happen again. Meanwhile, I'm going to start work on getting better locks for all our doors."

Li and Xochi headed upstairs to fetch her pillow, and then they went directly to his apartment.

2 Clouds

Logan Reid was in the kitchen making coffee when he heard Zoey tiptoe across his living room. She was coming from his bedroom to open his front door so she could return to her apartment before Charlie woke up. He turned and smiled at her. "Come back for breakfast," he whispered. Zoey grinned and nodded.

They had made this arrangement when they'd become lovers, and they'd been following it for a while. He'd given her the key to his place, and, almost every night, Zoey left her apartment and crept into his. The purpose of all the secrecy was to keep life as usual for Charlie. Logan didn't want to have to explain what he and Zoey did in bed together, which was so much more than sleep. Charlie was too young. So he'd suggested the arrangement, and Zoey agreed. Truth be told, Logan found it very exciting. This sweet, beautiful woman sneaking into his apartment and into his bed was the best thing ever.

Logan heard his cell phone beep. He took a quick look and saw a text from Detective Alvarez informing him that he would arrive by nine a.m. Logan responded affirmatively, then texted Li to tell him of the detective's arrival. He texted Marc, too. Time to wake up Charlie.

Half an hour later, Charlie and Zoey were sitting with Logan at his dining table, all three eating breakfast and discussing the day's plans.

"I'm going to a faculty meeting at the high school this morning," Zoey said.

"I'm going to summer camp today," Charlie grinned. "I like summer camp."

"I know you're going to be busy, Logan, so I'll take Charlie to catch the bus so he can make it to camp on time," Zoey added. "Then I'll go on to my meeting."

"Thanks, Zoey. I think the meeting with Detective Alvarez may go on a while. This is a rather strange and complicated situation. Xochi hasn't lived here very long, yet the break-in seems directed only at her. None of the other residents' apartments were affected, just Xochi's, and only one room in her apartment was trashed, not the entire place. This brings up a lot of questions." Logan turned to Charlie. "Looks like you're finished eating. Go brush your teeth. It's almost time to go."

"I'm going to go brush my teeth, too, Mr. Logan. Someone may want to kiss me."

Logan grabbed her and kissed her hard on her lips. "Come back, soon, Zoey Corban."

Only a few minutes later, Zoey and Charlie were gone, and Logan was cleaning up after breakfast.

* * *

Li woke up early. He stretched and took a deep breath. Bonita was on the pillow next to him, purring as usual. What to do today? Oh, yeah. His morning tai ji class had been canceled. Suddenly, he sat up in bed, eyes wide open. There was a beautiful woman sleeping on his couch! How could he forget that? *She* is what he would be doing today. Li thought he might just call in to work and tell them that he was sick or bored with his job or something. He didn't want to leave her. He wanted to stay and help Xochi.

He looked over at his clock, then pulled himself out of bed and headed to the bathroom. He quietly tiptoed into his kitchen after taking a peek at Xochi on his couch. She was snuggled in the blanket he'd given her last night, curly, long dark hair tousled against her pillow. She appeared to be sound asleep. So he went to the kitchen and made a pot of coffee. Maybe the scent of hot coffee would wake her up.

No. Still sound asleep. He sipped the coffee. She needed to wake up because that cop Logan told them about would show up this morning. How could he wake her up in a gentle way? Suddenly he thought of his guitar. Yes, some sweet, soft music on his acoustic guitar was called for. Maybe that would work. Li put down his cup, found his guitar, and sat down on a chair, not too close and not too far, from Xochi. He began playing one of his favorite tunes.

Xochi stirred, turned over, sat up, and yawned. She focused on Li, and watched him play. She sat quietly, concentrating on the music and on his fingers moving on the strings.

When Li finished the tune, he looked at her and smiled, "Want some coffee?"

"Sure. But more than that, I want to know what you were playing. Tell me about that tune. I love it."

"The tune is called '*Nuages.*' It's pretty old, written in 1939 or 1940 by a French Romani jazz guitarist named Django Reinhardt. Apparently he wrote it to express sadness at the Nazi occupation of Paris, and also to express sadness at the loss of a lover. It's an example of what's called "gypsy swing" music."

"That word, '*nuages.*' It's French?"

"Yes, it means 'clouds.' The lyrics are about how the clouds can darken the light of sun, and how the singer's heart could become dark, too, if he ever lost his lover."

"I heard you play earlier. You're really good." She smiled.

"Oh, gosh. Was I too loud?"

"No, I heard you late one morning. Almost everyone was gone from the building. It would have been okay with me if you were even louder. You play really well, and I love that tune."

Li's phone beeped, and he retrieved Logan's message. "We have to be downstairs at Logan's by nine. The detective will arrive then."

"I'll go get ready." Xochi rose and headed for the bathroom.

"Come back and eat some breakfast." Li set his guitar aside and went to the kitchen to heat up some left-over egg drop soup, and a couple of *baozi* on a plate.

When Xochi returned, she began sipping her coffee. "What's that?" She pointed to the *baozi*.

"*Baozi*. It's like a stuffed roll."

"Your cooking is very good, but I like your music even better."

Li was pleased to hear that. He was also pleased that she seemed so relaxed. She'd been really upset last night, and talking to the detective was probably going to be stressful for her.

They were almost finished with breakfast when Xochi looked at Li and smiled. "I know everyone calls you Li. But what is your real name? I mean, your entire name?"

"My Chinese name is Liang Li. Liang is the family name, and Li is my personal name. Family name comes first in China, and my parents immigrated from China. Also when I was born...," he paused, "I was born in California so I'm American, I mean a Chinese American. My parents gave me a western name, too, when I was born, which is David. So that's the name I use. David Liang for my driver's license, and passport, and credit cards and all that stuff. But everyone calls me, Li. You can consider Li short for Liang, or for my Chinese given name, Li." He grinned. "So are you sufficiently confused or shall I say it in Mandarin?"

Xochi chuckled. "I was just curious. I'll call you Li. It rhymes with "Lee." That's easy."

He smiled and nodded. Glancing at the clock on his stove, Li said, "I think it's about time for us to go to Logan's."

Xochi frowned. "Yeah." She stood up. "Here. I'll help you tidy up."

Five minutes later, they headed down to Logan's apartment.

* * *

Xochi, Li, and Marc were already waiting in Logan's apartment when the Tucson Police Department detective arrived.

Logan opened his door, stepped aside, and said, "Come on in, Detective." He gestured to a chair near where the others were sitting. "This is Detective Julio Alvarez. I'm sorry to say that he's had to visit us previously when we've had problems here. Turns out, he's a nice guy, and I trust him."

Detective Alvarez grinned. "Thank you, Mr. Reid. I trust you, too."

Logan continued. "And this is Xochi Navarro who had her apartment broken into, and David Liang, we call him Li, and Marc Tomassone. You've met these guys already." The three Casa Pacifica residents shook hands with the detective.

Li realized that he'd meet Alvarez only briefly earlier. He wasn't sure he would have been able to recognize the detective, so he took a closer look. He had the feeling that Alvarez had become an important person in their lives. He noticed that Alvarez was about Li's height, five feet ten inches, with a lean but robust build like a man who kept in shape. His dark hair and brown complexion revealed his Mexican heritage. Alvarez was smiling. Li was glad to realize that he felt comfortable in the detective's presence.

"Let's get started. This case seems to be a bit more complicated than a typical break-in," Alvarez said.

"Do you want to see the scene of the break-in?" Logan asked.

"Yes, let's do that first."

The four of them made their way up the stairs to Xochi's apartment. The door to the apartment was closed but unlocked.

Xochi looked at Alvarez and said, "We think the person who broke in must have picked the lock."

Logan nodded. "There's a locksmith coming later this morning to change all the locks in the building, including doors to the outside, front and back. As manager, I'm the only one who has a key to all the tenants' apartments, including Xochi's. The lock is changed with every new tenant."

They entered Xochi's apartment. Xochi gestured around her living room. "Nothing appears to have been disturbed here or in my bedroom." She led them to look into her bedroom. Alvarez took a good look around in both rooms. Then Xochi led him to the second bedroom.

"This is my studio." She stepped aside so Alvarez could enter the room. His eyes went wide as he stepped carefully through the debris to stand in the room. He looked back at Xochi.

"*Dios mio.* What a big mess! Can you tell if anything has been stolen?"

"No, I can't say for sure. But I kind of doubt it. My own artwork is stored in a chest in the living room, and I don't think it's been disturbed. What you're seeing is a lot of damage to my supplies."

"What's this white gooey liquid on different surfaces?" Alvarez asked.

"That's PVA glue. I mix it with methyl cellulose to make a special paste for book making. The methyl cellulose was dumped out, too. That's the dry powdery stuff you see."

"What about these papers? They don't look like regular typing paper or gift-wrapping paper."

"No, they are all art papers. This is a heavyweight paper for book pages, and some even heavier weight for watercolor or ink paintings. These colored and printed papers are mostly imports. Like these botanical papers in different colors were shipped to the U.S. from southeast Asia." Xochi pointed to a dark red paper with visible leaf inclusions. "That's mango paper. It came from Thailand." She stepped past a pile of papers, now torn and wrinkled. "That's origami paper from Japan." She pointed to an even more damaged pile. "And those two big rolls are this really fine paper I brought home from China. I hope I can salvage some of that."

Li's eyebrows went up. China. Xochi had visited China.

"These papers must be worth a fair amount of money," Alvarez said.

Xochi nodded. "I don't have a good accounting of how many papers I had altogether and what they are worth. I doubt my pitiful insurance will pay even a fraction of what I've lost." She turned to Li with a wan smile on her face. "But I'm going to do my best to salvage as much as possible."

Li nodded and said, "Good for you."

Logan turned to Alvarez. "Looks to me like the goal here was destruction, not theft."

Alvarez nodded. "I agree, unless you discover later than something other than your supplies has been stolen. Something valuable."

Xochi nodded.

"Let's take a closer look at that chest in your living room, and we can make sure none of your artwork was damaged or stolen," Alvarez said.

Xochi led them back to her living room. The chest was only about three feet high, and her television sat on the top. She pulled open the drawers one at a time.

"How valuable are these works?" Alvarez asked.

"Priceless," Li said.

Xochi chuckled. "Thanks for that, but if they don't sell, they are worthless."

Logan shook his head. "No. That can't be true, Xochi. If someone finds an unsold Picasso in an attic somewhere, that doesn't mean the Picasso is worthless. Far from it. Give us a general estimate of the value of these artist's books."

Xochi sighed. "Okay. When I do sell a book, it usually goes to a special collections library or a private collection. For my works, depending on size and complexity, and if the book is a one-of-a-kind or part of a small edition, the price goes from fifty dollars to five hundred dollars. Some artist's books are worth more, like over a thousand dollars each, and very occasionally, even more than that."

Alvarez nodded. "I don't see anything that appears to be damaged. Do you have a sense that all the books are still here?"

"I put them away in a certain order depending on size and shape so I could find a specific book easily. I don't see anything missing."

"Okay. Let's go back downstairs," Alvarez said. "I need to ask you some more questions."

Back in Logan's apartment, Alvarez started by asking Xochi, "So you just moved in here recently?"

"Yes. I had an apartment in the Sugar Hill neighborhood north of the University, but it was too small. I was teaching art classes, not just book arts but other arts, too, mainly relief printmaking and sometimes, beginning drawing. My apartment was too small for those classes, so I had to rent a space elsewhere for the classes, which got really expensive. And my apartment was too small for all my art supplies. My apartment here at Casa Pacifica turned out to be perfect."

"Have you had any conflict with fellow artists you are acquainted with here? Or a gallery owner you've had a relationship with?"

"No. I get along well with everyone. The artists here in Tucson are really supportive. I don't have any work in a local gallery."

"Are you the only one who teaches book arts?" Alvarez asked.

"No. There are a handful of others, mostly hobbyists. I often teach the more complex structures."

"How about previous students? Any problems with anyone?"

Xochi shook her head. "I can't think of any problems. The students all seemed quite happy with the classes that they took from me."

"I think Logan is correct," Alvarez said. "It does appear that the goal was destruction, not theft. Please make a list of students you've had in your most recent classes with their names and some general information about each one of them. And if you think of any reason why any one of them might be bent on destroying your supplies and equipment for any reason, make a note of that."

Xochi frowned. "I can't think of any reason why anyone would want to destroy my supplies."

"What if they wanted to be the go-to teacher for book arts in Tucson, and they viewed you as being in the way?" Alvarez persisted.

Xochi frowned. "I just don't know about that. I never got any bad vibes from anyone."

"Okay. Let's expand the field. Have you had any recent conflicts with any friends, associates, or even family members?"

Li was watching Xochi closely. That last question hit a nerve. She was looking at her hands, and it seemed to him that she had turned pale.

Now Xochi was gripping her hands tightly. She looked directly at Detective Alvarez. "I've had conflicts with my family for years. My half-brother is my biggest problem these days."

"Tell me about your family conflict and about your half-brother."

"Okay," she sighed. "I have to give you my family background. I hope I don't bore you all."

"Go ahead." Alvarez nodded his head.

"My mother is Mexican American. She was born and grew up in Tucson. She met this man from Sonora, Mexico, and they got married. She was living with him on a ranch in Sonora when she got pregnant with me. Then she found out he was seeing other women. Instead of accepting this as inevitable, she got really angry. They argued, and he hit her. That was too much for my mom. She left my dad and came back home to Tucson. They divorced soon after. I was born here."

"And then what happened?" Alvarez encouraged her.

"My dad remarried almost immediately and had a son. That's my half-brother. His name is Manuel Torres. They call him Manny."

"Your last name is Navarro?" Alvarez asked.

"That's my mother's last name. She stopped using the name Torres, and when I was born, she gave me her family name, not my dad's."

"So it's your brother you are having a conflict with?"

"Yes, but I think the rest of the family is supporting him. He wants me to marry someone he's chosen for me. I don't even know this dude that he wants me to marry. Manny has been pressuring me."

Li was completely surprised at this news. He and Xochi had the same problem: a family that waned them both to marry someone they didn't want or even know.

"Why do you think Manny Torres thinks he can choose the man you marry?" Alvarez asked.

Xochi looked at him, eyes flashing. "Because he's a total *pendejo*!" she cried. "He thinks because he's a man, he can tell me, a woman, and his sister to boot, what to do. He behaves as if what I want doesn't matter at all."

"But it's more complicated than that, right?"

"Yes, Detective, definitely more complicated. When I was a kid, my mother let me go across the border occasionally to visit family members, especially my cousins. After a while, she stopped that, and I've had only occasional contact with them since then, except for my half-brother hassling me. The last time I went across the border, I was a teenager. My mother told me once that they weren't good people, and it worried her for me to be around them. She wasn't sure I would be safe. Fact is, on my last couple of visits, I got that vibe, too. There were men, armed men, on my father's ranch. It was like they were protecting my father and the family. I got this cartel vibe. Like they were associated with a cartel, or in conflict with a cartel, or something. I have no idea, and I can't prove what I just said."

"What would be your half-brother's reason for you marrying someone he chose for you?"

"My guess is he's trying to create a bond between his family, my dad's family, and the other family, the family of the man they want me to marry. I did some research, and the man they chose for me, his name is Miguel Garcia, is definitely from a cartel-associated family." Xochi glanced around at all the men present. Logan, Marc, Li, and Detective Alvarez were frowning now, and all looked concerned. "My dad is really old now, and practically senile. My half-brother has taken over everything."

"When was the last time you heard from Manny Torres?" Alvarez asked.

"About a week ago. He wanted to bring Miguel Garcia to meet me. I told him no. I said I was too busy."

Alvarez nodded. "Trashing your studio could certainly be his attempt to put you out of business, and force you to consider his marriage proposal more seriously."

Xochi shook her head. "That's not going to work. I'm not giving up. I'll clean up the studio, salvage what I can, and keep on going."

Li nodded his approval.

"So you were downstairs in Logan's apartment when you heard a noise upstairs in your apartment?"

"Yes, we all came out to investigate, and that's when we saw a man running away. I guess he was a man," Xochi added.

Logan added, "Very likely a man, and roughly five ten or six feet tall, broad shoulders, dressed all in black with a hoodie and a black mask. Marc went out the front to stop him and I went out the back, but he quickly disappeared."

"Okay." Alvarez closed his notebook. "That's all for now. I'm going to try to find out more about Manny Torres and Miguel Garcia. Meanwhile, if anything changes, or if anything new comes up, contact me right away, Ms. Navarro."

"I will."

Alvarez turned to Logan, Marc, and Li. "Looks like you all need to be very observant in case something new happens. If you notice anything strange, contact me for that, too."

"Thank you, Detective," Logan said, as Alvarez rose and made his way to the door. "Our locks will be changed as soon as possible, and we'll all be watching out for anyone lurking around."

As soon as Alvarez was gone, Logan said, "Sorry, but we have to end this now. I have a busy schedule this week. Let me know if anything comes up."

Marc waved goodbye. "I'm doing some bird watching and photography. Then I'm cooking dinner for my lovely Angela when she comes home from work this evening."

Xochi turned to Li. "I'm going to get started on cleaning up the mess in my studio."

"If you need help, come and get me. And will you come to eat lunch with me?" Li asked.

"Sure. Will you play a tune for me?"

"If you wish." Li smiled. He leaned forward and kissed Xochi on her cheek. She smiled, and turned to go to her apartment.

3 THE NEXT STEP

Li was in his kitchen when he heard the knock on his door. He glanced at his clock. Twelve noon exactly. He went to open the door and found Xochi standing there, grinning at him.

"I was invited to lunch." She wiggled her eyebrows and smiled.

Li responded with his own wide smile. "Indeed you were. Please come in." He stepped aside and closed the door behind her.

"Do you want anything? Water, juice, some wine?"

"Water is good. I've been working hard."

"I can see. You have bits of paper or something in your hair, and your face is flushed."

"Oh, gosh." She brushed her hair back. "I guess I'm a mess."

"Sit down here at the table, and I'll bring us our lunch."

Xochi's eyes grew wide when she saw her plate. "That looks like *huevos rancheros*." She stared hungrily at the eggs and refried beans on tortillas covered in *salsa verde* and shredded cheese, with sliced avocados on the side.

"Yes, *huevos rancheros*. Are you okay with the *salsa verde* green sauce? I have some red sauce."

"I love *salsa verde*. This looks fabulous."

Li sat down and picked up his fork. "Dig in, Xochi."

Several mouthfuls later, after many expressions of praise for how delicious the food was, Xochi sat back and sighed. "You are a great cook, Li. But I thought you cooked Chinese food."

"I do. That's my job. But I get tired of it sometimes. I'm an American, and I like a lot of variety in my diet like most Americans. Mexican is one of my favorites."

"What else do you like?"

"Indian food, Greek food, Brazil has some great dishes, and I like new things. I like to eat."

Xochi laughed. "I do, too."

"How's the cleanup going?"

"Better than I thought. I'm sorting everything out, and I'm putting similar things into piles in the living room. Then I'll move them back into the studio once I get rid of the damaged stuff. Actually it's not as bad as I thought. Some art papers are destroyed, and I'll have to buy more PVA glue. I only have a small container left. But things could be worse. I'm glad it wasn't a fire. That would have been a disaster." She hesitated. "I'm going to need a little help with something."

Li nodded. "No problem. I'd be pleased to help you."

"One of the shelves in the closet needs to be put back in the right place. You're way taller than me. I can't reach that high up to put it back in place, but I bet you can."

"Sure. After lunch, let's do that."

"Could I please hear another tune first?"

"Yes. Any requests?"

"No, play what you want. I know it will be good."

Xochi made herself comfortable on the couch, and Li sat near her, guitar in hand.

"You'll recognize this one." He began playing "Summertime."

She closed her eyes and hummed along. "I love that song." She sighed. "Before I go back to work, will you play the cloud song again?"

Li began playing. When he strummed the last note, he sat quietly for a moment, then looked at Xochi. She was looking at him with an expression on her face that he couldn't really identify. Maybe questioning. She wanted to know something, but would she ask him?

Xochi sat back and looked away. "I guess I'd better get back to work."

"I'll go with you and put that shelf in place."

Li followed Xochi to her apartment. He glanced around and saw, just as she'd described, the living room floor had organized piles of art materials. She went directly to her studio, and he followed her. At least now, they could walk across the studio floor without stepping on things.

"Here." She handed Li a shelf. "This is the only one I can't reach."

He took the shelf, entered the closet, lifted it, and began placing it on its metal support bracket. He glanced up and saw another shelf, narrower than the lower shelves, that was very high against the back of the closet. He could barely see a box far back in the shadows on this shelf.

"Do you need this box? I doubt you can reach it."

"No, it's just some stuff my mom gave to me when she moved to California. She said it was mostly a few old books that her granddad left to her when he died, my great-grandfather, I mean. He told her to pass them on to me if she didn't want them, and she said that I should have them since I'm the book nerd. I haven't even opened the box."

"Your mother lives in California?"

"Yes, she got remarried when I was a student at the university. She and my step-dad live in La Jolla, north of San Diego."

"And siblings?"

"No. How about you?"

"No. I had an older brother, but he died."

"I'm sorry. An accident?"

"He was killed in an earthquake in Sichuan Province. He was visiting China at the time."

Xochi frowned and shook her head.

"I guess I'd better go now so you can get back to work," Li said.

"I don't want to work. I want to go home with you. Hear more music. Talk with you. I like you."

Li was surprised at how pleased he was to hear that. "I like you, too. How about if I play some recordings of Django Reinhardt? You can hear the original '*Nuages*.'"

They returned to Li's apartment, and he put the music on. They sat quietly together on the sofa, listening.

"There's more to this story," he told her. "I read somewhere that this tune became sort an unofficial anthem in France during the Nazi occupation. The tune expressed the French people's hopes for liberation."

"That makes sense."

They fell quiet again.

Li spoke first. "I don't want to be a bummer, but I'd like to know if you've started that list of students that Detective Alvarez wants?"

"Only in my head. I have to write the names down."

"Will you give me a copy? I'd like to share it with Logan, and see what he thinks. He's more than our manager. He's very good at solving mysteries. Your list might have a clue. He may actually know someone on the list. He knows a lot of people."

"Sure. I'll do that. But you know, I'm pretty sure the detective thinks my half-brother is involved."

"Yes, if your half-brother is being an ass and is trying to force you into a marriage you don't want, then trashing your place might be a very big message from him to you. I've been thinking that maybe you need some help with defending yourself. Have you ever had a self-defense class?"

"No. I'm not very big. You think I could defend myself?"

"Yes, I do. You have the spirit. I suggest when you think you have the time, let me know, and I can help you learn the basics. I have some training."

"Okay. That sounds good."

Li began to strum on his guitar. This time the song was, "Tucson Train."

Xochi grinned. "That's a Bruce Springsteen song."

Li nodded. Xochi sat quietly, listening. When he completed the tune, they sat looking at each other, smiling.

Finally Xochi spoke, "I have to get back to work. But before I go, I think we should take this to the next step."

"Count me in. What's the next step?"

"I invite you to dinner."

"Sure." He grinned. "What are you going to cook?"

"Me, cook?" She laughed. "No way. We're going out to eat."

"Make it a place where I won't be recognized. I called in sick this morning, and I don't want anyone to tell on me. And while we're eating together, I'd like to hear about your trip to China."

"Okay, it's a done deal. I'll come back for you closer to dinner time." She stood up on her tiptoes and kissed him on his cheek. "See ya later." And she was gone.

Li sat for a long time, holding his guitar and smiling.

* * *

The locksmith came early and changed the locks first on the outer doors to the Casa Pacifica apartment building, then he began changing locks on individual apartments. Logan watched as he worked, and asked a couple of questions about the reliability of the locks. Because the front and back doors would be locked at all times, anyone visiting would have to ring the doorbell and hope someone heard it and came to open the door. Logan would have to get a key for the postal clerk to make regular deliveries to the mail boxes inside.

After the locksmith left, Logan sat in his favorite chair and stared out the window thinking about recent events. He couldn't help but feel disturbed. After several years of peace and quiet, Casa Pacifica Apartments seemed to have become the target of one illegal act after another. He was concerned about his role as manager. Was he doing something wrong? Maybe not being observant enough? He couldn't really figure out what his shortcomings might be when it came to managing the apartments. Okay, granted the bad guys were never residents of Casa Pacific. But there were always ties to the residents. He didn't know what to make of it all.

Time to get the day going. First, he needed a shave. He had to go to a meeting later that afternoon and see his new office and meet everyone in the department's office. He would be teaching two classes, and he'd be available for office hours if students wanted to see him. He wanted to look presentable when he met everyone. A beard was okay and clean-shaven was okay, but a scruffy mess was not okay. Scruffy was popular now, but not for Logan. He headed for the bathroom only to stare in the mirror there.

Zoey. She often came into his thoughts. He didn't know what to do about her. A couple of days ago, she used the phrase "our family." Maybe she was talking about the Casa Pacifica family. But he didn't think so. He was almost certain that she was speaking about him and Charlie and herself as "our family." Truth be told, that's how he thought of her, too. She was part of his family now. He loved her. Charlie loved her. Why didn't he take the next step? Tell her how he felt, and ask her what she thought about marriage?

Logan continued to stare at himself in the mirror. After brooding over his life for the past three years, he'd come to realize that he'd been traumatized by his wife's sudden death, more than he'd ever realized. He was self-reflective, and he knew himself well enough to recognize that he was afraid Zoey would die like Caroline had died if he loved and married Zoey. His wife Caroline, and Charlie's mother, had a sudden and deadly brain aneurysm when Charlie was only two years old. Her death changed everything. And Logan was changed forever. He also knew he was being totally irrational to be afraid that marriage to him would kill Zoey, but he felt paralyzed about moving forward. "You're a chicken shit," he muttered.

He heard a knock on the door. "Come in." It was Zoey. "You don't have to knock."

"I know. I just don't want to startle you. Are you shaving?"

"Yes."

"Can I watch?"

He looked at her with a question on his face. He chuckled. "Sure, but why do you want to watch?"

"I'm just curious." So she watched him as he lathered his face and began to run the razor over his cheeks and chin. She was smiling the entire time.

"So what do you think?" Logan asked her.

"I'm glad I'm not a man. I don't think I would like doing that every day. It looks dangerous."

He grinned. "I'm glad you're not a man, too, but for different reasons." Finished now, he washed his face, dried it with his towel, splashed on some aftershave, then he kissed her. "Let's go sit on the couch, and you can tell me what you've been up to."

"Logan, aren't you supposed to graduate soon? When is the graduation ceremony?"

"Friday afternoon. I sort of forgot about it. My parents were going to come, but my dad got hurt mountain biking near their home in Durango. I think I told you already that they moved to Colorado when my dad retired. He's got a brace on his leg now, his ankle is broken and in a cast, and he's having trouble getting around. Mom is making him use a wheel chair until he gets better. So they won't make it for my graduation."

"Your graduation ceremony is important. You've earned a PhD. That's a big deal. So let's not forget about it."

Logan shrugged his shoulders.

Zoey persisted. "Think about Charlie. You'll set a very good example for hard work and persistence. I'll sit with him in the audience, and we'll be so proud of you when you receive your diploma. Please, Logan."

She rarely asked for anything, and this was an easy request to fulfill. He just had to walk across the stage in a cap and gown and accept his diploma in its protective cover. No big deal.

"Okay. If that's what you want."

"Thank you, Logan."

She took his hand in hers, and looked at him directly in his eyes. "Logan, I want you to know that I've taken our relationship very seriously."

Oh, no. Logan was alarmed. Past tense. Has she given up on me? he asked himself. Does she want to break up?

"I want you know that I admire you, and I trust you completely. You're my best friend."

Okay. This is sounding a little bit better. "I feel the same about you, Zoey." He squeezed her hand.

Zoey frowned. "I've decided that the next step in our relationship is for me to tell you more about my past, my son, and my former husband. This won't be easy for me."

He'd been wondering about this for some time, but he figured Zoey would tell him when she was ready. Looks like now was the time.

"Okay. Go at your own pace. I'm listening."

"I was born and grew up in Minnesota. I went to college at the University of Minnesota in the Twin Cities, and that's where I met this boy. His name was Brad. I should say 'man,' but we were both young. And he never grew up. He was the first guy I ever had sex with, and I thought I had to marry him because we had sex. So we got married. We earned our degrees, and we both got jobs. I was a biology teacher like I am now. I got pregnant pretty fast, and Josh was born nine months later."

Logan nodded. He could see the tears in her eyes now.

"Josh wasn't very old when he was diagnosed with cystic fibrosis. Do you know anything about this disease?"

"Not much," Logan said.

"It is an inherited disease that causes damage to the lungs and other organ systems. These days, some folks can grow to adulthood if they are given the best care. Not Josh. He always had a hard time breathing. The doctors and nurses and I took care of him as best we could, and toward the end, I spent my days and nights in the hospital with him. Over time, Josh went downhill, and he died when he was only three years old. I was heart broken. He was the sweetest, smartest little boy." Zoey sighed.

"I'm so sorry, Zoey." Logan put his arm around her shoulders.

"That's why I enjoy Charlie so much. He's like Josh. Smart, sweet, and totally lovable, but thank god, Charlie is healthy. He's wonderful." She sighed again. "So when Josh died, I was already on my own. My husband had gone off somewhere months earlier, and he never came back. Just before he left, he told me that he hated his life with me and Josh, and he'd had enough. He was finished with us. Later, his lawyer contacted me with divorce papers, and I signed them."

"For the best, don't you think?" Logan asked.

"Yes. For the best. You are a hundred times the man than he was."

Hearing that really pleased Logan.

"You'll be interested to know that I had genetic tests done on me because of Josh's condition. There's no trace of cystic fibrosis in my DNA. Josh's disease came from his dad's side of the family."

He knew what she was saying. She could have more children without the worry of that inherited disease. Logan pulled her closer. "You're very brave. I admire you."

"I love you, Logan," Zoey whispered. Her eyes were full of tears now.

"And I love you, Zoey." Okay. There. He'd said it. Maybe he wasn't such a chicken shit after all.

"I guess I'll go pick up Charlie from summer camp now. He can stay with me until you get back from your meeting."

"I appreciate that. Charlie will be pleased to know that Gwenny the greyhound is coming to stay with us this evening. Marc and Angela are going to the movies. Maybe the three of us could take Gwenny for a walk."

"Great idea! That will make Charlie happy."

Zoey left, and Logan sat thinking about what his next move should be. Maybe he should have a man-to-man talk with Charlie. Yeah. That's the next step.

* * *

Xochi knocked on Li's door in the late afternoon. He answered immediately.

"Are you ready to go stuff your handsome face?" She grinned. "We're going to the Tanque Verde Swap Meet."

Li laughed. "Yes. I'm ready. Are we going shopping at the Swap Meet?" He had expected a restaurant. He had no idea what Xochi was up to now, but he was sure that he couldn't wait to see where they would eat.

"We can shop later if you want to." She leaned over and patted his knee. "But you're hungry so let's eat first. We're going to visit Comida Park which is on the grounds of the Swap Meet. Do you know what the word '*comida*' means?"

"Something to do with food, I think. I'm not sure. I need to learn Spanish."

"Yes, you do. '*Comida*' means 'meal.' There are a bunch of food trucks in Comida Park, about twenty the last time I looked, although the total number changes from week to week."

"Wow. That's a lot of food trucks. What kind of food?"

"Several Mexican trucks. One is Asian-American. We can avoid that one if you think you might be recognized. Have you ever eaten a *pupusa*?"

"No." Li laughed. "What the hell is a *pupusa*?"

"It's the national dish of El Salvador. It's a griddle cake made of rice or wheat flour, and with all sorts of good stuff in between the cakes or piled on top."

Li shook his head and grinned. "I'm started to feel culturally ignorant. I've never heard of that, much less eaten it."

"Okay. Let' start with *pupusas*, and then check out the other trucks."

"If there are twenty trucks, I'll be so stuffed by the end of the evening that I won't be able to walk."

"Don't worry. I'll take care of you."

They were quiet for a few minutes.

Li spoke first. "Oh, wait. I forgot to mention. I told you I thought you should learn some self-defense, and I would teach you. But I think you should take a class with an experienced teacher and with classmates. Almost always, your fellow classmates will be women, so you can connect with them, too."

"You don't want to teach me?"

"You should learn from a teacher who knows what he's doing. Or she. Anyway, if I try to teach you, I'll become disturbed."

Xochi frowned. "What do you mean, 'disturbed?'"

"In a self-defense class, if I teach you, I'll probably have to touch you a lot to help you position yourself, and to interact with me physically, and that would be…"

"Disturbing?" She had a quizzical look on her face.

"Bad choice of words. Not 'disturbed.' More like 'stimulated.'"

Xochi laughed.

"How about this? After you've taken some self-defense classes, you can try out your skills on me. I'll pretend to attack you, and you can defend yourself."

Xochi laughed again. "This is starting to sound like a lot of fun."

"Let's hope so." Li looked away, embarrassed now. He probably shouldn't have said that about being stimulated, although she didn't seem to mind. In reality, she was a real turn-on as far as he was concerned.

"Okay, Mr. Potentially Stimulated. Let's go eat!"

They headed for Comida Park.

4 CONFLICT

When Xochi pulled her car out onto the street and headed east, Li couldn't help but notice a car parked across the street from Casa Pacifica Apartments. He looked from his side window and saw that as soon as he and Xochi moved forward about a block, the car had left its parking place and was following them. Or was it following them? He wasn't sure.

They went east to Alvernon Way, then south to Palo Verde Road, which was a major route from midtown Tucson to the airport. But instead of going all the way to the airport, Xochi turned off into the Tanque Verde Swap Meet. Li glanced back. The car, a dark red Nissan, was still there, but several cars back. Li wondered if he was being paranoid. The Swap Meet was a popular destination, and Palo Verde Road was heavily traveled. He decided to stay vigilant. Xochi found a parking place, and they exited her car at the Swap Meet.

"Let's just walk around Comida Park first so you can see all the trucks. Then we'll focus on getting you some Salvadoran food."

Li nodded. He looked back. Yes, the red Nissan had just turned into the Swap Meet grounds. No, he wasn't being paranoid at all. They were being followed, and he would definitely be keeping an eye out.

Li and Xochi entered the Swap Meet area known as Comida Park, and they began strolling around surveying the food trucks parked there. Li stopped at several trucks to read the menus posted on the side of the food trucks.

"Oh, look! There's Lebanese food," Li said. "We're definitely coming back for that another day." They continued strolling. "There's the Asian-American truck. Looks like it's Vietnamese."

"So that's probably safe for you."

"Yeah. For sure. No one will tell on me for skipping work. And I saw several Mexican places. There's one focused on American food. I'm curious about what they call 'American.' Could be anything. Okay, Xochi. We're eating Salvadoran this evening, but we'll be back again and try something different."

Xochi laughed and took his hand in hers. "You like to try new things."

"I do." He swung their hands together between them.

Finally they came to the one known as *La Pupuseria*.

Li looked at the menu. "Oh, boy, this is going to be hard. I don't know what to choose."

"Try one of everything. We can take leftovers home with us."

Li stepped up to the opening and spoke to the young woman behind the counter as he pointed to the menu. "Okay. I'd like one each of *pupusada*, *revueltas*, *chicharrón y queso*, *calabaza con queso*, and *espinaca con queso*." Li turned to Xochi. "I hope I said all that correctly. That's plenty to eat."

"And I have a bottle of wine in my bag." Xochi grinned. "Let's find a table and eat."

Li intentionally seated himself so that Xochi would be facing him, and he could see anyone who tried to approach her.

"You'll have to tell me what we're eating. I know some of the dishes but not all. I've sort of been stuck in Chinese cuisine for a while."

She smiled and shook her head. "You've lived in Tucson several years, and you've never explored all the options? You are so culturally deprived. *Pobrecito.*"

"What's a *pobrecito*?"

"Poor thing. Poor baby."

Li chuckled. "Okay. That's true. I'm a sad case."

"I'll explain everything so you can know what you are eating." She retrieved the wine from her bag, along with two small glasses. She poured the wine, and handed him a glass.

"To stimulation," she said, with a smile.

Li grinned. "To stimulation." They began sipping their wine. "You're kind of a naughty girl, aren't you?"

"I certainly hope so." She wiggled her eyebrows.

"Before I forget, I'd like to hear about your trip to China."

Xochi nodded. "My mom always wanted to travel, and I had the travel bug, too. We decided to go on a trip to China in celebration of my graduation from high school and because I won an art scholarship to the University of Arizona."

"Good for you."

"We flew to Beijing, took a train to cities farther west, Xian and Chengdu, and then we took a tour on a boat on this big river to a town called YiChang. Then we took the train all the way to Shanghai."

Li nodded. "The big river is called the Yangtze in the West, but the Chinese call it the Chang Jiang. It actually forms in the mountains of Tibet, and then it flows all the way to the East China Sea and the Pacific Ocean. Only when it approaches the China Sea is it called the Yangtze."

"We stopped along the way everywhere, and we went to two kinds of places."

"Historical sites?"

"Yes, and markets. The tour guide gave us plenty of opportunities to buy Chinese goodies."

He shrugged. "You were tourists."

"Yeah, we were marked. Tourists, and even worse, American tourists. Oh! There was a third spot. Restaurants. We ate a lot."

"What did you think of China and the Chinese?"

"Some places are very beautiful. I found the historical sites to be fascinating. But my mom and I realized that we were sort of captives on a tour. We decided to return someday by ourselves, no tour, and do some real exploring."

"I'll take you on a tour. My tour will definitely be an exploration."

"And stimulating?" She wiggled her eyebrows again.

Li laughed. "There's that naughty girl again."

"I don't know about the Chinese people. We rarely interacted with them. The tour guide spoke English so I talked to him, and the vendors in the market were mainly focused on selling us stuff. That's one reason why I'd like to return. It would be fun to meet some regular, ordinary Chinese people. The only other thing I could say about the Chinese people is that there are a lot of them."

Li nodded. "One point four billion in the People's Republic."

The food arrived, carried on a large platter by a teenage girl. Xochi immediately began explaining the individual dishes, their ingredients, and how they were made. Li asked questions, and Xochi elaborated.

Once they began eating, Li shook his head and grinned. "Delicious! I like everything."

Finally, Xochi put down her napkin and said, "Enough! I can't eat anymore." She looked at Li and smiled. "What brought you to Tucson anyway?"

"I wanted to get away from home and try something new so I came to Tucson to go to university. My degree is in history."

Xochi shook her head. "History? So relevant to cooking."

"Yeah, I didn't know what I wanted to do, and I always found history interesting. I had a part-time job in one of the Chinese restaurants during my student years. My parents jumped on that. They said they'd pay my way to a chef school in Shanghai if I would agree to go. So I went. I lived there for six months, then I came back to Tucson and started working as a chef full time."

"So your parents wanted you to be a chef?"

"No. They just wanted me to do something to make a living. I'm the second son. My brother was the first-born son. He had all these expectations placed on him to fulfill his first-son duties. He'd finished his engineering degree, and he was going to get married. Then he was killed in the Sichuan earthquake. His death meant that the first-son expectations landed on me. I'm supposed to have a career, find a good woman and marry her, produce kids, move back to southern California, and take care of my parents."

"But you don't want to do all that?"

"No, I'm kind of a bohemian type, I guess, and that kind of regimented life doesn't appeal to me. I mean, I'll definitely take care of my parents when they are old, but the rest of it…," He shrugged.

Xochi nodded. "I totally get that. I'm kind of like that, too. If I'd lived back in the 1960s, I would have been a hippie. But I'm lucky because I'm living the life of an artist, which is what I always wanted. My biggest problem is convincing my *pinche* brother to leave me alone."

"*Pinche*? That's a bad word, isn't it?"

"Yes, I curse a lot."

"What does that word mean?"

"I'll be polite." Xochi batted her eyelashes. "It rhymes with 'clucking' or 'ducking.'"

"Got it," Li chuckled. "So you are a naughty girl, and you're a modern-day hippie, too?"

"Yes, and you are a bad boy bohemian." She returned his smile. "You know what? Nina told me about you before I moved in. She said you are a ladies' man."

"Uh oh. What does that mean?"

"You like women, and you like flirting with them." She was laughing now.

Li grinned. "Guilty as charged. Maybe it's a good thing that Nina has moved to Vancouver. If she'd stayed, she would be here to tell tales on me."

Xochi nodded. "She liked you a lot. She said you were shot by some guy who was after her."

"Yeah, the gunman went after Nina's band members, too. He confused me with one of them. I think it was her drummer. I'm not sure. Anyway, I'm okay now."

"You're okay now except that you are not sure you want to continue being a chef, right?"

Li frowned. "That's one problem. Worse is that my parents have chosen a girl for me to marry. She lives in China, and she barely speaks English. I don't know her at all, and I certainly don't want to marry her."

"Whoa. We have the same problem, then. We both have family members trying to force us into marriages we don't want," Xochi said.

Li nodded. "Speaking of that, Xochi, please look at me and continue looking at me because I'm going to tell you something that may be upsetting to you. Can you do that?"

She stiffened and sat up straight. "Yes, I can do that."

"A man in a Nissan followed us here from the Iron Horse neighborhood and into the Swap Meet. He's sitting at a far corner behind you. We won't be able to get to your car without going past him."

Xochi was frowning now. "What does he look like?"

"Mexican. Dark hair. Mid-to-late twenties. About my height, maybe five ten. Dressed in a dark suit and white dress shirt. No tie. He's nursing a beer, and he's been staring at us and scowling the entire time he's been sitting there."

"That sounds like my brother Manny." She was frowning, and her jaws were clenched. She reached down into her purse and pulled out a small portfolio of photos. She handed one to Li. The photo was of a large group of people. She pointed to one man.

"Yes, that's him," Li said.

"Damn." She looked down at her empty plate, then up at Li. "I'm sorry to get you mixed up in this." She put the photos away.

Li smiled at her. "You're worth the trouble, Xochi. Don't worry. He's not that big or tough. He looks like a guy who's used to having his way, mainly because he has money, and he usually has some pals with him to back him up."

"That's Manny exactly. He's made a lot of money in recent years, probably all illegal. I mean, I really think he's trying to solidify relations with a cartel family so he can make more money."

"But right now, he's alone." Li smiled.

"He could hurt you."

"Or I could hurt him." He grinned.

Xochi giggled. *"Ai, que macho!"* Her smiled disappeared. "Let's be careful. Seriously. I don't want you to get hurt."

Li nodded. He began stacking their cardboard food containers together, then he stood up and threw everything in a nearby trash bin. "Come on, Xochi. Let's go home."

Xochi stood, Li took her hand again, and they began walking toward the parking lot.

Manny stood up, still scowling. He approached and growled. "Xochi, you're going with me. Time to go home."

"Leave me alone," Xochi said angrily.

Li nodded. "Leave my girl alone."

"Who the hell are you?" Manny glared at him. "She's going with me. She is *not* your girl." He reached out and grabbed Xochi's wrist and began pulling her away from Li. Xochi resisted. She managed to jerk her arm hard enough that Manny was pulled forward.

Li stepped up and put himself between Xochi and Manny. "Let her go." His voice was calm but firm.

"You stay out of this," Manny yelled. He raised his right arm and launched a punch toward Li's jaw.

But before the punch could land, Li shifted his body to the left, raised his right arm, which was bent at his elbow now, and he blocked Manny's punching arm. Li grabbed Manny's arm and twisted it toward the left. Then he took Manny's hand in his to force it backwards. Li continued twisting, which caused immense strain on Manny's wrist and elbow. Manny gasped in pain, but he could not move out of Li's grip. Li moved forward, closer to Manny's body, and with his other arm he shoved Manny roughly to the ground.

Manny glared up angrily at Li.

"Let's go," Li calmly said to Xochi. They began walking at a moderate pace back to her car.

Xochi reached out and took his hand. "I'm so, so impressed. Was that some of the Chinese martial arts you were talking about the other day?"

He nodded. "Notice that I went toward him, not away. When you pull away like you did, it makes it easier for him to stay in control. If you go forward toward him, you have a better chance of getting out of his grip and then doing some damage to him by getting him off balance. It will surprise him, too, to have you moving toward him."

Xochi nodded. "It's like that old saying. 'The best defense is a good offense.'"

"That's right. That's why you need to take a self-defense class. You need to learn the basics."

She nodded again. "I'm convinced." She squeezed his hand. "You've just impressed the hell out of me, Li."

He laughed. "Good. I want to impress you. But even more, I want you to like me."

They were back to her car by now. Xochi stopped him before he got into the car. She put her arms around Li's neck and quickly kissed him on his cheek. "Thank you, Li." She looked at his eyes directly. "I do like you. And I liked it when you called me your girl."

Li smiled. "Thank you for the delicious dinner. Now let's go home."

* * *

Later that afternoon when his son returned from camp, Logan gave Charlie a sliced banana and some orange juice for a snack. "Charlie, Zoey has gone off for a little while. I need to talk to you about something serious."

Charlie looked at his dad with a frown on his face. "I've been good."

"I know you have. This is not about your behavior. It's about you, and me, and Zoey. But this is a man-to-man conversation, father and son, just between you and me. You're five years old now. You're old enough to discuss this with me. You have to promise that you won't tell anyone what we talk about here, especially don't tell Zoey."

"I promise. I'm almost six."

"Okay. This is serious." Logan took a deep breath.

Charlie began eating. He watched Logan with a frown on his face. "Did something bad happen?"

"No, not at all. I'm thinking something good might happen. That's what I want to talk to you about. Charlie, Zoey loves us. She loves you, and she loves me."

"Yeah, I know. Zoey told me that."

"She told you that she loves me, too?"

"Yes. She said that. She said she loves you, and she said she loves me. I love her, too."

"Well, that's what I want to talk about. I love Zoey, too. I'm thinking maybe Zoey and I should get married. She'll be my wife, and she'll be your mom. What do you think?"

Charlie put his orange juice down. He grinned. "Yeah! That's a great idea." He jumped up from his chair, came around the table, and hugged Logan. "Yes, please. Ask Zoey to marry us! We'll be happy."

"Good. Then we agree. I'll start shopping for an engagement ring to give her." If she wants it. He frowned. Would she want it? He thought maybe yes. Probably yes. Definitely yes.

"I want to give her an engagement ring, too. I'm going to make a ring for her. Or maybe a necklace. Yeah, a necklace. An engagement necklace. That's the best."

"Good idea." Logan sat back in his chair. This was easier than he'd anticipated.

Charlie went back to eating his snack.

"Do you have homework or anything you need help with?"

"I have two worksheets. One is numbers, the other is letters."

"Show me."

Charlie went to his room and returned with two papers.

"See this one. It has numbers. I have to color the correct number of whatever is in that row. Like this one." He pointed. "The number is nine so I have to color in nine apples. Not eight. Not ten." He pulled out the other sheet. "This one has three boxes that are the letters that make a word. Two of the boxes are filled in with letters already. I have to put the correct letter in the first box to make the right word. There's a picture above that shows you the word."

"I see. There's a picture of a cat. The boxes below have 'a' and 't' and you have to fill in the correct first box."

"That's right. The answer is 'c'. That makes the word 'cat.'" He giggled. "It's easy."

"You're a very intelligent young man. You're learning to read."

Charlie came around the table again and hugged his dad. Logan held his son against his chest for a long minute.

"Okay. You go to work, and I'm going to read my book. When Zoey comes home, we'll make dinner."

Charlie nodded. "I have to find my crayons first."

"And remember our secret. Don't say anything."

"I won't!" Charlie ran to his room giggling. He returned quickly and began working on his homework.

Zoey arrived not long after, and she and Logan decided on what to make for dinner.

Suddenly there were noises at both the front and back staircases. Logan smiled. "Sounds like everyone is coming home at once."

Three minutes later, they heard a scratching at Logan's door. "Charlie, go see what that is." He turned to Zoey and said in a low voice, "I bet that's Gwenny scratching to get in." Zoey grinned and nodded.

Charlie threw open the door. "Gwenny!" He laughed as Gwenny the greyhound entered the apartment and began licking Charlie's face. Her tail was wagging vigorously. "Gwenny, I love you!" Charlie gave Gwenny a hug and said, "*W⊠ ài n⊠!*" He got more doggy kisses in return.

"Charlie," Logan said. "You better take Gwenny back to Marc and Angela so she can get some supper. Then she's coming to stay with us for the evening."

"Come on, Gwenny," Charlie said, as he began to run up the front stairs. At the top, he and his favorite dog found Li and Xochi at the entrance to Li's apartment, and Marc and Angela at the entrance to their apartment. They were chatting with each other.

"Hi, Charlie," they all said at once.

"Marc, my daddy says Gwenny needs some supper, then she's coming to stay with us. We're all going for a walk."

"Yes, that's the plan. Angela and I are going to the movies this evening."

"Hey, Charlie," Xochi grinned. "I haven't seen you in a while. What are you doing these days?"

"I'm doing my homework," Charlie answered. "And I'm going to make an engagement necklace. My daddy is going shopping for an engagement ring, and I'm making an engagement necklace."

Li chucked. "Engagement necklace? Are you getting married?"

Charlie suddenly fell silent. His smile disappeared and a stricken look appeared on his face.

"It's a secret. I can't tell."

Xochi and Angela exchanged smiles. Li and Marc had knowing looks on their faces. Both men were trying not to laugh.

"Okay. You don't have to tell," Xochi said. "But if you need any help, let me know."

"Thank you, Xochi," Charlie said seriously. "I have to keep this a secret."

"Are you going to tell Zoey?" Angela asked. She glanced at Xochi who was grinning now.

"Oh, no! I can't tell Zoey. I promised my daddy to keep this a secret."

"Good for you, Charlie," Angela said. "I know your daddy is very proud of you."

Marc intervened. "Enough of this or we'll be late. I want to feed Gwenny, and Angela and I need to eat a bite." He turned to Li and said, "Do you two want to go see a film with us tonight?"

Li looked down at Xochi. "Sure, are you okay with that?"

"Very okay," Xochi grinned.

Marc turned to Charlie. "Okay, you go home. I'll bring Gwenny down to you in about twenty minutes. I'm going to feed her some supper now."

Charlie nodded, turned away and ran down the hall to the front stairs. The adults heard him descend the stairs in an especially noisy fashion, and slam his home apartment door behind him.

The four adults all turned to each other and laughed softly.

"This is a secret, y'all. Don't tell." Angela wagged her finger. "Especially you boys. Keep your mouths shut."

Xochi nodded. "Yes, a secret. And when Logan and Zoey announce their engagement, act like you're surprised."

They all laughed.

5 A LIST

Li woke up the next morning and, almost instantly, his head was filled with competing thoughts.

His job. He had to go to work later that afternoon because he couldn't continue to claim that he was sick. He groaned. His job. Too much stress and for no good reason. The new manager was a total pain in the butt. Li's thoughts turned again to the food trucks at Comida Park. He'd noticed that all the food truck workers were smiling, and they looked like they were enjoying themselves. Must be great to make your own hours and decide on your own if you want to open or not on any given day, Li thought. Yes, a lot more freedom. No annoying-as-hell manager in your face. Freedom.

Remembering his trip to Comida Park with Xochi turned his thoughts to her. To Xochi. She was on his couch again. Yeah, the lock to her apartment had been changed, but Li couldn't help but feel worried. He had this nagging sense that something wasn't right. He couldn't shake the feeling that she was in danger. The encounter with her half-brother Manny at the food truck park had convinced him that the dude wasn't going to let her go so easily. Li figured that too much money was involved, and Li couldn't always be there to protect her. He found it easy to imagine the brother forcing his way into her apartment somehow, maybe drugging her, and hauling her back across the border where he'd keep her captive and force her to marry a man she'd never even met. No, he couldn't let that happen.

So last evening after they returned from the movie theater with Marc and Angela, Li turned to Xochi and said, "Come with me for a minute." She followed him into his apartment.

"Xochi, do me a favor, will you?"

"What's that?"

"Please sleep on my couch again. After what happened, I just feel like...," Li shrugged his shoulders. "I don't know. I just have this feeling. What if your brother shows up again?"

Xochi smiled. She reached out and touched his chest. "I have a new lock and key."

"I don't care. That bastard brother of yours is the type to break in and take you before I could get there. Please, Xochi."

"On one condition."

Oh, lordy, she was a piece of work. He couldn't help but grin. "What's that?"

"I'll sleep on your couch if you'll play your guitar for me in the morning."

Li smiled now thinking about her. He glanced over at his guitar tilted against the wall. Time to get up, make some coffee, and play a new tune for her. He stretched, pulled himself out of bed, and threw the covers in place in his feeble attempt to make up the bed. He wasn't really into house keeping. He made his way to the kitchen and started the coffee. Then he retrieved his guitar, sat down in his favorite chair only a few feet away from Xochi, and he began strumming softly.

Xochi turned and sighed.

Li glanced up. Her eyes were open, and she was looking directly at him, a smile on her face.

"I like that one," she said softly. "But I like everything you play."

Li chuckled. "Not very selective, are you?"

"I'm selective. I know good when I hear it. You're good. Every tune is good."

"Thank you. Now it's time for you to get up. We have to go down to Logan's apartment and meet with the detective this morning. I want to tell him what happened at the food truck park. And he asked for a list of your recent students."

Xochi sighed. "Oh, yeah. I forgot about that." She threw the blanket back and stretched. He noticed immediately that she'd taken off her bra. Unconstrained. Soft. Curvy. Li could see everything and imagine even more. He ducked his head down and looked at the strings on his guitar. Oh, crap, he thought to himself, I mustn't stare at her. But the fact was, she was delectable, delicious, so very, very touchable. And so unlike any woman he'd ever known. The word "feisty" came to mind. Sweet and tart. Tasty. He put his guitar down and headed for the kitchen. He could hear Xochi on her way to the bathroom. He decided to start breakfast.

Twenty minutes later, they'd had their coffee and a simple breakfast.

"So how about that list?" Li asked.

"It's in my head, and on my computer, I have a complete list of the students in my last two classes with contact info for each student and a little about each one. Let's go to my apartment, and I'll print out the list."

"Sounds good." He paused. "Xochi, sometime soon, could we go back to your place for a while? I'd like to learn more about what you do. About artist's books, I mean. I don't know anything about them, and I'm really curious. Not today. I have to go in a little early to work today. Maybe tomorrow."

"I'd love to show you some artist's books, mine and some other artists, too." Xochi paused. "So you're going to work? And you work late, right?"

"That's right. I won't be home until around eleven p.m."

"Maybe tomorrow? I have a lot of artist's books, and I'd love to show you the different structures."

"That would be great."

They took the short walk down the hall to Xochi's door. Within a few minutes, she had her computer up and running, and she printed out two copies of her recent students' names and information. Li looked around while she was busy with printing. Everything looked fairly tidy. He peeked into her studio room. Most of the art supply items that had been on the floor were now back on shelves. He noticed large rolls of intensely-colored botanical papers placed on upper shelves. Xochi called to him when she'd finished printing her list. Five minutes later, they were downstairs knocking on Logan's door.

"Come on in," Logan said, when he opened the door. "I just got a text from Detective Alvarez. He'll be here in just a few minutes. Need anything? Coffee? Water?"

"No, thanks," both Xochi and Li answered. "We just ate," Xochi added.

The bell to the building's front entrance rang. Logan clicked on a button to let Alvarez in. Only a minute later, they heard a knock on Logan's apartment door, and Logan opened the door. "Hey, Detective, good to see you. Come on in." They all sat together at Logan's dining table.

"Okay," Alvarez began. "You have a list of past students?"

"Yes," Xochi said, "but first, I think Li and I should tell you what happened to us yesterday. We went to eat dinner at Comida Park at the Tanque Verde Swap Meet grounds. My half-brother showed up. He's the one I told you about."

"Actually, he followed us," Li added. "He was parked across the street from Casa Pacifica when we drove away in Xochi's car. He followed us all the way to the Swap Meet."

Alvarez frowned. "This is the half-brother who lives in Sonora?"

"Yes. We had just eaten, and we were going to leave when Manny confronted us. He grabbed me and tried to force me to go with him. But Li did this Chinese martial arts move on him and knocked him to the ground." Xochi reached out and patted Li's hand.

Alvarez's eyebrows went up, and he grinned. "So we have a martial arts expert living here?"

Li shook his head. "No way am I an expert. Sorry to say, I'm definitely an amateur, and what I did was an easy move. My intent was just to get his attention and make him realize that he shouldn't be handling Xochi like that." He looked at Xochi. "I'm recommending that Xochi take a basic self-defense class for women."

Alvarez nodded. "Good idea. Every woman should take a self-defense class." He paused and said, "About the break-in at your place, Miss Navarro, I also have to mention that one of our forensic officers dusted for fingerprints when the team was here, but he found so many prints from so many people that I think they probably won't be very helpful. I'd need to get your brother's fingerprints to ID him for sure."

Xochi nodded. "My students, friends, everyone in Casa Pacifica, too, lots of people have been in my apartment. There's just too many."

"Okay. For now, let's go over your list. I want to make sure we cover all the bases."

"I assume you only want students from recent classes? I've only taught two classes since I've been here in Casa Pacifica Apartments."

"That's right. Since the damage to your apartment was done recently, I think it's safe to conclude that a recent student may have been involved. Maybe." Alvarez frowned. "Again, everything points to your brother, but we don't want to be unhappily surprised."

Xochi nodded. "I'll go over the class that I taught first, right after I moved in. There were four students in each class. I don't have room for any more than four at a time." She handed Alvarez one of her printouts. "First on the list is Lisa Merrick. She's an art teacher at one of the local high schools. Not Zoey's high school. I think it's on the east side of Tucson."

Alvarez nodded. "Next?"

"The next two, Jenny Wilson and Crystal Clark, are both teachers and colleagues at the same school in midtown. Jenny is the high school art teacher, and Crystal works with disabled kids. And the fourth teacher, Renata Martinez, teaches art at a high school on the south side of Tucson."

"Give me your impression of the four," Alvarez said. "Did anyone seem to have anything on her mind other than the class work?"

"All four were acting like they were on vacation and having fun. We laughed a lot. All four are in their late twenties or early thirties. We didn't talk about personal lives much, but I did learn during our time together that all four are married, and one teacher, I think it was Jenny, has two kids of her own." Xochi pointed to the paper in Alvarez's hand. "You'll see each teachers' social media links, and info about each one on their school websites. I got the impression that each one is interested in doing her own artist's books, and also teaching book arts in her classroom."

Li spoke up, "I'm surprised that book arts can be taught to disabled kids."

"From what Crystal said, it depends on the level of disability. In my class, she focused a lot on the simplest forms, mostly simple folded structures. I'll show you some of those."

Li nodded.

"Of course, when it comes to decorating the pages of the book, and I use the term 'pages' loosely, any kid knows how to make marks on paper." She grinned.

"So you didn't sense anyone with a hidden agenda or a complaint or anything?" Alvarez asked.

"No. Like I said, they all acted like they were on vacation and having fun."

"How about the other class, the most recent one?" Alvarez asked.

Xochi handed him a second piece of paper.

"The first one is Guadalupe Lopez, but we called her Lupe. She's friends with Renata Martinez, but she teaches art at a south side middle school. She learned about this class from Renata so she signed up. She said Renata told her that the class was a lot of fun, and Renata said she learned a lot, too."

Li smiled. "You're getting a good reputation."

"I hope so!" Xochi grinned. "These three are Erika Baker, Ashley Hall, and Brian Parker. The two ladies are older and retired. My guess is that these women were in their sixties or early seventies. Brian wasn't that old, maybe early forties."

"How did they learn about your class?" Alvarez asked.

"There's a nonprofit arts organization here in Tucson that focuses on paper arts. By that I mean any artwork

on paper or made of paper. They all belong to that organization. My take on the women is that art has been a
lifelong hobby. Now that they are retired, they can focus
on doing fun art things that they've always wanted to do.
I'm not sure about Brian. He didn't talk very much."

"What do you know about their past lives?" Alvarez
asked.

"Erika worked in real estate, Ashley worked for an office supply business, and Brian was an accountant."

"So they were here to have fun, too?" Alvarez smiled.

"Yes, and they did have fun. They didn't giggle quite as
much as the teachers, but we did have a relaxed and fun
time."

Alvarez nodded.

"We mostly talked about art and about different arty
things happening in Tucson, like what is going on at the
Tucson Museum of Art, different galleries, local artists'
open studios and stuff like that. No one had any com-
plaints or seemed to have an issue."

Logan smiled. "Your classes sound like fun."

Alvarez nodded again. "Yes, they do sound like fun.
Okay, I'll check out their social media, school websites,
and anything else related. But it's looking more and more
like your brother is the problem." He stood up. "I'll let
you go now. Thanks very much for the additional information."

Xochi stood up, too. "Thank you, Detective Alvarez.
You're the best!" She turned to Li, grabbed his hand, and
pulled him to his feet. "Come on, lazy boy," she said.
"You're going with me." Li was grinning when Xochi
pulled him away. They closed the door behind them.

Just before he left, Alvarez turned to Logan and said,
"I have something else to ask you. Something personal."

Logan followed him into the hallway, and closed the
door behind them. "Sure. What's on your mind?"

"I'm looking for a new place to live. The owner of my apartment complex just sold out, and the new owners are going to completely remodel the complex and turn the place into up-scale rentals."

"And the new apartments will be more expensive, no doubt," Logan said.

"Rumor has it that the rents will be doubled. Or even more. I won't be able to afford that."

Logan shook his head. "It's all these out-of-state folks moving here. They're driving the prices up." He thought Alvarez looked a little nervous. "So you're wondering if we'll have an opening here at Casa Pacifica?"

Alvarez's eyebrows went up. "Yeah. This would be a convenient place for me to live so I can get to my office on time. And the rent for a one-bedroom is pretty reasonable. I looked you up on the web. Do you have any openings coming up? And would you mind having a cop live here?"

Logan chuckled. "We had an FBI Special Agent here for a while. I think we could handle a Tucson Police Department detective."

Alvarez grinned.

"I don't have an opening right now," Logan continued, "but I think we will very soon." He was thinking of Zoey. Of course she would move in with Charlie and him if she agreed to marry him. Of course.

"I have until the end of the month to find a new place. Sooner would be better for me to have the new place available. I could take my time moving, and my departmental duties won't be disrupted."

"No problem. I should know within the next few days if we'll have a place for you. I think you'll find that you fit in well here, Detective."

"I guess it's time for us to be a little less formal. You know my name is Julio Alvarez, but everyone calls me

Chito Alvarez. 'Chito' is a common Mexican nickname based on slang. It has several meanings, but in my case, I think it means to hush or be quiet. I'm the youngest of eight children in my family. I guess I had to make a lot of noise to get any attention when I was a kid so my older brothers started calling me Chito and telling me to shut up. My mother is the only one who calls me Julio."

Logan stuck out his hand. "Nice to meet you, Chito Alvarez."

Alvarez grinned. The two men shook hands. "Okay, I have to go back to work now, and get started on this list. As I said, it seems very likely that Xochi's half-brother is the one causing all this trouble. But I want to be thorough and cover all the possibilities."

As soon as Alvarez left, Logan retrieved notes for his first class tomorrow. He looked over the notes, then stopped for a while, thinking about the next day. He decided that after his class, but before he returned home, he would go shopping for Zoey's engagement ring. He knew she was an admirer of Native American art, and especially Navajo jewelry. So that's what he would get for her. Not a diamond ring. He'd get something really special that he knew she would love. Silver and turquoise. Yeah, he thought to himself. He was going to get her something she couldn't say "no" to. He laughed at the thought.

* * *

Xochi held Li's hand and pulled him back to his apartment.

Li laughed, "What are you doing?"

Xochi stopped and looked up at him. Li immediately noticed there were tears in her eyes.

"What's going on?" He was mystified.

"I'm sorry, Li. Just talking about this with the detective made me sort of scared. The idea that someone was in my apartment and tearing up my art supplies just scares me. I want this to be over. I want to go back to work, to be an artist again, and to pester you every day." She smiled wanly.

Li pulled her close, his arms around her. "Don't worry. This will be over soon. I'm going to take care of you." She tilted her head against his chest. He hoped with all his heart that he *could* take care of her. For now, though, he wanted to cheer her up. "Meanwhile, let's go have some fun."

"Fun?" Xochi looked at him, her face brighter now.

"Yes, let's go to Comida Park again and get a snack. I'd like to take a closer look at those food trucks."

"Really? Okay, count me in."

Off they went. When they arrived at Tanque Verde Swap Meet, Li took Xochi's hand, and they went on a tour of the park. But this time, instead of looking at menus, Li walked around each truck, both the open-for-business and the closed trucks. At one point, he took a small notebook and pen out of a back pocket, and made some notes.

"I think I know what you're doing," Xochi said, grinning. "You're thinking about opening your own food truck."

Li nodded. "Think I'm crazy? I have a good job, and it's secure. Most people would think I'm nuts to give it up. I know I won't make as much money if I do this, but that's okay. I just don't know if I can even afford it. I bet these trucks are expensive."

"Yes, you can look into it. But I think a food truck could really work for you. You're not happy now. You like to cook, but you don't like your job. You're more of a bohemian type who likes to do his own thing. You think maybe if you worked for yourself and had your own food truck, you'd be happier. And happy is better than wealthy."

Li smiled. "Yep. You're very insightful, Xochi Navarro."

Xochi looked at Li, her eyes wide. Her flirtatious, feisty demeanor had disappeared. She was serious now. "I feel like I know you, Li. I mean really *know* you. I think we are the same kind of people. I really, really like you. I want you to be happy. I want to help you be happy. If you want a food truck, I'll do what I can to help."

Li felt very moved at her words. Xochi was special. "I really, really like you, too. I would be grateful for anything you can do to help me."

At the food truck park, they wandered around, and Li continued to take notes. He stopped often to ask questions of anyone working at an open food truck. Finally, he turned to Xochi and said, "Time to go home. I have to go to work."

When they arrived back at Casa Pacifica Apartments, Li asked Xochi, "Do you want to stay in my apartment while I'm gone? Would you feel safer?"

Xochi frowned. "I have work I have to do. I have an exhibit coming up, and I haven't finished my art pieces." She grew quiet for a moment. "What do you think about this? I could spend the afternoon in my apartment, then when evening comes, I could go stay in your apartment until you come home? I'll bring a book or watch your television."

"That's a good idea. I have an extra key I'll give you."

"It's a deal."

Half an hour later, Xochi was back at work in her studio, and Li had gone off to his restaurant dressed in his chef's white clothing.

6 Requests

Logan woke up early. Today was the day to start his new job teaching, and the day to shop for an engagement ring for Zoey. He pulled himself out of bed, showered, woke up Charlie, fed them both breakfast, and then walked with Charlie to catch the summer camp bus.

Just before Charlie got on the bus, Logan bent down and hugged him. "Charlie, you have fun today, and remember to keep our secret."

"I will, Daddy." He jumped onto the bus and joined a group of boys sitting in the back. He turned and yelled, "Bye!"

Logan returned to the apartments, collected what he needed for his class, dumped his backpack into his car in the back parking lot, and he headed for Pima Community College's West Campus. He took deep breaths trying to calm himself. He was nervous. Okay, so it's a new school, and a new department, and he didn't know anyone except those administrators who had interviewed him. And new students, too. No need to be nervous, he told himself. He liked teaching. He especially liked teaching philosophy. He always thought that students who signed up for a philosophy course were really special. They weren't thinking of how to make a living like business or engineering majors, they weren't thinking of how to do something like nursing or art, they were just there to explore something new. New ideas. He liked that in those students. Yeah, this would be good. A good day. A good job. Zoey popped into his mind. A good wife. A good marriage. A good family. A good life. Yeah. He was doing the right thing.

Several hours later, Logan was back in his car and driving away from the college campus. Everything had gone very well. Extremely well. He met several colleagues in the Art, Humanities, and Communications Department, and all the staff in the offices. Everyone was very friendly and welcoming. Early in the afternoon, he met his first class. There were nineteen students. They all seemed open to him and were even brave enough to ask questions. Logan was very pleased.

The only thing at all that was bothering him now was the break-in and damage to Xochi Navarro's apartment. He couldn't help but feel that all the residents were a little bit less safe if someone could get in that easily. He just hoped to hell that the new locks on every apartment would put an end to any more break-ins. And the idea of having a cop living in Casa Pacifica was a real plus. "So stop brooding, Logan Reid," he muttered to himself. This day had gone really well so far. Enjoy it.

Next task: an engagement ring. He drove directly to the jewelry shop that specialized in Native American jewelry artists. It didn't take him long to decide on a delicate yet solid silver ring with a lovely, oval-shaped turquoise stone in a nice setting. He couldn't help but notice a special wedding band nearby, slightly wider than the engagement ring. The wedding band was silver with inclusions of small turquoise stones around the entire ring's outer surface. Then he saw a second ring, very similar, but wider. Perfect for a man. Maybe matching wedding bands? He shook his head. Don't get ahead of yourself, he thought to himself. One step at a time. Logan purchased the ring along with a small ring case. He headed home.

* * *

When Li returned to his apartment on the previous evening, he found Xochi sound asleep on his couch. She had an open book on her chest, an art book. He gently lifted the book from her hands and moved it to the coffee table, then covered her with her blanket. He turned off the lamp next to the sofa, and he went to bed, but it was a long time before he could go to sleep.

His life had been calm and uneventful for a long time. Well, not really. He was shot in the shoulder when that nutcase had gone after his friend Nina, the jazz pianist. But the bullet had missed Li's main shoulder joint and had only broken the end of his collar bone. He healed pretty quickly. He had a job that was okay for a while, although it was getting more stressful now. He had that side gig of modeling men's clothing. That was fun, mainly because of all the hot girls that were models in the photos, too. And he had a casual girlfriend, Laurel. She didn't ask much of him but regular sex. That was what he wanted with her. Nothing serious. Just fun.

Then Xochi Navarro showed up. Everything changed. Yes, she was the target of some kind of something. It wasn't clear what the perpetrator was doing. Maybe trying to scare her. That might be her brother trying to scare her into doing what he wanted. Or someone looking for something to steal. What? The really valuable stuff, the artwork, was there and safe. Maybe someone had a grudge against her and just wanted to cause her a lot of trouble by smashing up her studio and destroying her supplies. If so, who, and why?

Yes, a target. She was a target. And Li felt very protective of her. But it was more than that. He found her intriguing and irresistible. Sweet and tart. So smart. He wanted to go to the next step, but he wasn't sure she was interested in him. He felt unsure of himself in a way that he hadn't felt in forever. Li sighed. Just take it step by step. You'll figure it out, he said to himself. He finally fell sleep.

Now it was morning again.

He heard Xochi stirring while he was making coffee. "Ready for a coffee?" Li called to her.

"Please." Her voice was soft, sleepy.

Li came into his living room and handed her the coffee. "I'll fix you breakfast in a minute. Then we can go to your apartment. Remember? You're going to introduce me to artist's books today." He sat down and smiled at her. She looked only half awake.

Xochi rubbed her eyes. She looked at him, smiled and shook her head "no."

"No?" Li asked.

"Music first," she croaked. "I can't survive without your music."

Li chuckled. "You know how to say the right thing."

"You talk too much." She was smiling at him now. "Play first. Then you can talk."

"Yes, ma'am." He reached for his guitar.

Li started with some soft, slow tunes, then picked up the pace with a little more energetic songs. After about twenty minutes, he said, "Okay, that should get you started. I'll go fix us some breakfast now."

This time, he cooked some noodles *al dente*, then added some sesame sauce and pickled vegetables.

"Yum," Xochi said after a big bite. "Weird, but yummy."

"Weird?"

"I don't even know what these vegetables are."

"Mainly cucumbers and some other lesser known veggies, like summer radish. This is a Korean dish."

"Oh. That's nice to know." She made a face.

Li laughed. He felt like teasing her. "Don't you know how to cook? Anything at all?"

She looked him directly in the eye. "Hell, no. My idea of cooking is to find the nearest food truck. My goal in life is to find a man who can cook and play music, preferably at the same time."

Li laughed. "I'll have to work on playing and cooking at the same time."

"Do that, and I'm yours."

He felt a lurch in his heart. He was warm all over now. He didn't know what to say. The idea of Xochi being *his* thrilled him.

Xochi looked up at him. "Let's tidy up and go take a look at the artist's books."

They went together to her apartment door. She unlocked it and headed directly for her storage units in the living room. She turned to Li and said, "Here. Take these into my studio room, and I'll be there in a minute with more."

Li followed her directions. His hands were full so he used his elbow to flip on the overhead light in the studio. Xochi soon followed. They sat down together at the table, the artist's books spread out in front of them.

"Okay. I'm going show you examples of different categories of books," Xochi started. "We'll start with something really simple." She reached out for what appeared to be a thick roll of paper with bamboo on the ends. "This is a scroll." She opened it up. The paper was delicate and very long, maybe three feet long. There were beautiful forms that looked sort of like writing but not in a language or script that he recognized. Also he could see ink images of trees painted on the paper.

"This is beautiful. It kind of reminds me of old scrolls I saw when I was in China in different museums. What's the writing? I don't recognize it."

"Actually that's an example of what we call asemic writing. It looks like some established form of writing, but it's really an art form with no meaning, no real words, and no real message except the beauty of the shapes. This is a fairly recent scroll by an artist who was inspired by the old Chinese scrolls, and he has replaced Chinese characters with asemic writing."

Li nodded. He'd never seen anything like asemic writing.

"Let's move on to books that are slightly more complex. First are the fold books." She reached out for a couple of examples. To Li, they looked very different from each other. One was very colorful with wild abstract images and a few words. The other book had a combination of printed words in English and a few images. Subtle.

Xochi opened the sample books. She glanced over at him. "See how when I open these up, you can see they are one big piece of paper that has been folded."

"Oh, I see. Sort of an accordion shape."

"Exactly. In fact, that's what this fold is called. Accordion. But look at this one. It's one big piece that has been folded in half first, then into accordion folds, then a cut was made along the fold, but only in the middle." She folded it together, and it looked quite different. "This is called a maze structure."

Li nodded and smiled. "You make it look simple."

"Actually, it is a very simple structure. Look at this one. Hold it and look at it carefully."

He turned it in his hands. "Okay, I see the accordion fold but the fold is pretty narrow...or tight. I'm not sure what to call it. I'm guessing that the two sides of the accordion are hidden in the front and back covers of the book. But what are all these little rectangles of paper attached to the accordion folds? They look like little flags going opposite directions."

Xochi reached out and patted his hand. "Clever boy. That one is called a flag book." She reached for another book and handed it to him.

Li took it in his hand. "This one has two big folded books attached at each end. And one fold has cut out shapes in it so you can see what's on the other fold."

She handed him another one. "Similar structure but a very different effect."

This time the pages were attached to accordion folds on each side, each page was cut out, and he could see through each one all the way to the back of the book. She reached for a second book with the same structure, but it looked quite different.

"Cool!" Li grinned.

"These two are called tunnel books."

"That's a good name for them," he said.

"Here's something similar but different. This is called a popup book. See how the levels are not attached to an accordion fold, but attached to a central heavier fold."

"Okay. I see. I think there are some kids' books like that."

"Yes, manufactured children's books. Of course, artist's books are either unique or in small editions of maybe three or five. Are you getting overwhelmed?"

"No. I'm kind of fascinated now. It amazes me how you can take something that starts out with such simplicity and turn it into something unique and beautiful."

Xochi grinned. "Kind of like the chords you play on your guitar?"

"Really?"

"Really. Yes, simple and beautiful. You don't value your music as you should, Li."

Li sighed. She was right. Music was something he did for love. Was he devaluing it because he figured the music would never make him any money?

"We artists do our art because it's a spiritual calling." Xochi looked into his eyes. "This isn't about making a living." She laughed. "Although we do have to figure out how to make a living."

He didn't know what to say. She was describing exactly how he felt.

"Just so you know, my great-grandfather left me some money when he passed on. It's enough to pay my rent for a while. I'm trying to build a reputation not only as an artist but also as a teacher. I had a gig teaching at Penland School in North Carolina last summer. I hope for more opportunities like that. I'm going to teach at a center for book arts in California in a couple of months. And I continue to teach locally. Teaching improves my reputation as an artist, too, and I get more sales of my works. I'm hoping that by the time my inheritance runs out, I'll be able to support myself."

Li nodded. "You already have a good reputation here. Think of those students that you described to the detective."

"Thank you," she said. "Okay. Time to move on to stitched bindings."

"Stitched? Sewing? Yikes. I don't know how to sew."

"Wait 'til I get through with you." She grinned. "This is a pamphlet stitch. See how we stitched this little pamphlet into the fold of a fold book. It's easy."

Li nodded. "I see several pamphlets stitched into that one."

She handed him another book. "This is called an Oriental or Japanese binding. Tell me what you see."

He held the book in his hand, opened it, and turned the pages. "Looks like a pile of pages that are poked over here on the left side between the covers and then sewn together. The stitching looks pretty simple."

"Good. And now this one."

"Whoa. This one is much more complicated. There's all this fancy stitching on the spine of the book." He opened it. "And each of these groups of pages are folded and stitched into the spine. Or something. I'm not sure how to describe what I see."

"You're doing just fine. We called this a codex binding."

He held the book in his hand, then he turned to Xochi. "I have a request."

"Oh, yeah, what's that?"

"I'd like to make a book. I want to start with something really simple. I like that scroll you showed me. Do you mind teaching me or should I sign up for one of your classes?"

"You don't need a class for a scroll because it's so easy. We can do that now if you want."

Xochi found a couple of bamboo sticks in a drawer. "Go choose some paper, Li." She gestured to one of the shelves. "I suggest something light weight that will roll up easily. See that one?" She pointed to a roll of paper about three feet tall. "That's Japanese Unyru paper. There's a similar paper made in Thailand, too."

"Perfect." Li pulled the roll down. The paper was white with tiny gold metal flecks on the surface. It was very delicate.

"Here. I'll show you the proper way to cut a length of it for your scroll," Xochi said. "We're creating what's called a volumen scroll. You unroll it left to right. The other way is to hang it up and read it from top to bottom. That's called a rotulus scroll."

In only ten minutes, Li had created a long scroll with bamboo sticks on each end. He sat back in his chair and chuckled. "My first book. Now I just need to figure out what to put on this very long scroll." He looked over at Xochi. She was looking at him intently, a serious look on her face.

Li frowned. "What?"

"Why are you so circumspect?" she asked. "I thought you'd be all flirty and stuff. Like Nina said, you are supposed to be a ladies' man. But you're not like that with me. You are sweet and funny and sometime very serious. I don't know what to make of you."

Li shrugged. "I guess I'm this way because of you. You're not what I expected. Don't ask me what I expected. I don't know. I just know you are really special."

Xochi smiled. Their eyes locked. After a long moment, Xochi said, "You want to kiss me, don't you?"

Li smiled.

"But you're not sure." She grinned. "You don't know what I'll do. Maybe I'll slap your face and kick you out of my apartment. Or maybe I'll throw my arms around you and kiss you intensely."

Li's eyebrows went up and his smile grew.

"So what's it going to be?" Xochi teased.

Li leaned in and kissed her softly on her lips.

Xochi threw her arms around him and began kissing him passionately. After a long moment, she pulled back and said, "Enough of this."

"I didn't get enough." He smiled. "I want more."

"More later. Now you have to do something with your scroll. Do you want to paint on it or write on it or both?"

Li nodded and frowned. "I'm not sure. I think maybe write on it in Chinese characters."

"Oh wow! You can write Chinese characters?"

He nodded. "My parents wanted to make sure that their sons didn't lose their heritage. My brother and I both speak, read, and write fluent Mandarin. Or past tense for my brother. I told you that he's gone now."

Xochi nodded. "Maybe you could teach me some simple characters."

"Sure. We'll use a special brush and ink for that. But not today. I have to go to work in a little while."

Xochi sat back in her chair. Then she sat up straight. "Oh! I forgot. Remember that box on the high shelf that I couldn't reach? My mom told me that my great-grandfather left me a few of his favorite books. One of them was supposed to be a Chinese scroll."

"You never looked in the box?"

"No. I loved my great-grandfather a lot. He was really good to me. I was afraid I would just start crying looking at his books. I knew I would look at them someday." She stood up. "Today's the day!" She moved over to the closet. "Could you please get that box down for me?"

"Sure." Li stood up, went to the closet, and retrieved the metal box. He handed it to Xochi. She placed it on the table and opened it. Inside were several antique books. One was a scroll wrapped in a piece of leather.

"Wow. These look really old, Xochi. Maybe they should be in a museum." He glanced over at Xochi. She had tears in her eyes.

"Do you want to open the scroll and see what's there?" she asked.

"I don't want to damage it. I'll try, but we may need to take it to some expert. Seriously. This is very old." Li removed the leather cover. He began to unroll the scroll, slowly and carefully. Xochi leaned over his shoulder.

"The script is old, too, not just the paper. We're looking at old-style characters, not modern at all. I can make out a few words. The red ink stamp indicates that the author was a Mandarin for the emperor. The Mandarins were the administrators of the emperor's empire. This looks like it might be Ming Dynasty." He looked at Xochi. "Yes, let's find someone who can help us. I don't want to damage this." She nodded her agreement. He wrapped the scroll in its leather again, placed it in the box and put it back on the high shelf.

"This has been fun, Xochi, but I have to go to work now."

"I'm teaching a class tomorrow morning. I only have three students. Want to come?"

"Sure. I'll pay you for the class."

"No, you won't. You've been nothing but good to me. You stopped my *pinche* brother from dragging me off. You give me good things to eat and a safe place to sleep. Best of all, you play music for me. No way are you going to pay me for a class." She frowned and shook her head.

Li laughed. "Okay. You'll be in my apartment when I come home tonight?"

Xochi nodded. "I will."

He leaned over and kissed her gently. "See you later."

* * *

Logan picked up Charlie at the bus stop that afternoon.

"Did you have fun today?" he asked his son as they walked home.

"Yeah, we played games, and also we had a craft class. We got to choose clay or we could use what the teacher called 'fibers.' I chose fibers today, and tomorrow we'll trade places. The clay kids will do fibers, and the fiber kids will do clay. I chose fibers because we could make things out of strings and ribbons. I made Zoey an engagement necklace."

"You did? That's great, Charlie!"

"It's made out of these tan-colored string things that my teacher said is something called 'yarn.' And the teacher gave me a bead to put where the two ends come together. It's a big red bead. The teacher said it was dyed coral. What's coral, Daddy?"

"It's something that normally lives in the ocean. I'll look it up, and you can see some photos. Also I want you to know that I already found Zoey an engagement ring. When she comes this afternoon, I think it will be a good time to ask her to marry us."

Charlie grinned. "Okay!"

They went home, and Logan brought Charlie his afternoon snack, orange juice and a banana. He was just finishing his banana when Zoey knocked on the door.

"Come on in, Zoey," Logan called. "Want a snack?"

"No, thanks." Her eyebrows went up as Charlie made a dash for his room, calling out, "Hi, Zoey."

Logan followed Charlie and closed the door behind him. "Okay, Charlie. I'll go first. I'll ask her, and then it will be your turn." Charlie nodded, giggling the entire time.

Logan returned to the living room with Charlie on his heels.

Zoey was sitting on the sofa. "What are you two boys up to?" she asked affectionately.

"We have a request, Zoey," Logan said. He knelt down on one knee and pulled the ring case out of his pocket. He opened it and held it toward her. "Zoey, I love you. Will you be my wife?"

Zoey gasped.

Charlie stepped up, giggling and bouncing on his toes. "Zoey, I love you. Will you be my mom?" He handed her the necklace that he'd made.

Zoey burst into tears. She croaked out a "yes," and then she sobbed even harder.

Charlie looked at Logan, confusion on his face. "Daddy, Zoey's crying. Is she unhappy?"

"No," Logan grinned. "I'm pretty sure she's happy."

"Why is she crying?"

"It's a girl thing. Sometime girls cry when they're happy. I don't really know why. I can't explain it." Logan reached for Zoey's hand. "Everything is just fine, sweet pea."

Zoey found a tissue and wiped away the tears. "I'm sorry. You surprised me." She looked at Logan. "I love you, Logan. Yes, I'll be your wife." She looked at Charlie. "I love you, Charlie. Yes, I'll be your mom."

Charlie placed the necklace around Zoey's neck. Logan took the ring from the case and placed it on Zoey's finger. Then they both sat on each side of Zoey, their arms around her.

"Thank you for honoring our request," Logan said softly.

7 A Surprise

Li started the day again with coffee and more music for Xochi. She always seemed so pleased to wake up to the soft sounds of his guitar. He liked that.

Xochi stretched and sat up. "Okay, you woke me up in the proper manner. Thank you very much. Now I need to get going because my class will start at nine this morning. I need to be there for the students. And you should be there, too."

Li laughed. "I will! I will! And you'll have to open the downstairs door so they can get into the building."

"Right. That's kind of an inconvenience, but I guess it will keep intruders out."

"Let's hope so. I'll go make us some breakfast."

"And play your guitar at the same time?" She giggled.

"If that ever happens, you won't be going anywhere except…" Li glanced at his bedroom door.

"Oh, you naughty boy." Xochi laughed again and headed for the bathroom.

Li sighed with relief. He wasn't sure how forward he should be with her. She seemed okay with his suggestive look.

Twenty minutes later they were in Xochi's apartment getting everything ready for her class.

Xochi paused, looked at Li, and asked, "Are you really interested in making artist's books? Why are you taking my art class?"

Li shrugged his shoulders. "I'm curious." He paused and looked at her directly. "And I wanted to be with you."

Xochi breathed out. "That's so sweet. I want to be with you, too." She smiled. "I feel like kissing you right now. But we need to get everything ready."

Li chuckled. "Business first. Pleasure later."

Xochi grinned. "Don't forget that…later, I mean." She looked over at her shelf of supplies. "Let's get the cutting pads out first."

Li helped her arrange the craft cutting pads around the big table, one for each student.

"What the hell is a craft cutting pad?" Li asked, frowning. "What are these lines on it?"

"The lines help you keep your cuts straight. A cutting pad is made of heavy PVC. I think that's a plastic something. Yeah, polyvinyl chloride. Anyway, the pads are self-healing so you can cut paper, and if the razor blade in your razor knife goes into the pad, it will close up and heal itself."

"Razor knife!" He looked at her with a terrified expression. He bit his lip so he wouldn't laugh.

Xochi laughed. "Don't worry. I won't let you cut your fingers off."

"Are you sure? I like my fingers."

"Stop teasing me." She came around the table and kissed him on his cheek. "You're such a weeny!"

Li grabbed her and gave her an intense kiss on her lips.

"Stop it!" She giggled again. "Get serious. Remember? Business first."

"And pleasure later."

Xochi nodded. The front doorbell rang. She turned to run out of her apartment and down the stairs. She returned in five minutes with three young women. Li guessed they were in their early twenties.

"Everyone have a seat, and we can introduce ourselves. First, you know me. I'm Xochi Navarro, I'm a book artist, and sometimes I paint, too." She gestured to the young woman next to her.

"Hi, I'm Emma Francis. I'm an art student at the University of Arizona." She glanced over at Li and batted her eyelashes.

Li grinned. Xochi rolled her eyes.

The young woman sitting next to Emma said, "I'm Madison Clark. I'm an art student, too, at the UofA. And I have a part-time job at a bar. I can make a mean margarita." She looked at Li, smiled and wiggled her eyebrows.

Li heard Xochi sigh heavily.

"And I'm Olivia Rodriguez. I'm an art student, too, at the UofA, but enough about me." She turned to Li and said, "Tell us who you are."

Li grinned. He heard Xochi groan and say in a barely audible voice, "Oh my god." He bit his lip again. Not laughing was becoming a challenge. "My name is Li. I'm a cook."

Xochi shook her head. "He's actually one of Tucson's top chefs. He's won a bunch of prizes."

The three students squealed. "Oh, tell us where you work. We'll come and eat your delicious food!"

"You like Chinese food?" Li smiled.

"Yes!" They all said at once.

"I'll make something special, just for you three. I'll give you a business card." He glanced at Xochi. Li was amazed at how they all squealed and giggled in response to nearly everything he said. It was difficult not to laugh.

Xochi stood up. "Okay. Enough with the introductions. We need to get started now. Did everyone bring the tools I listed for you? Metal measuring ruler? A utility knife with a new razor blade? Also needles of different sizes?"

The three women nodded and pulled their tools from backpacks. Li looked at Xochi, a question on his face.

"Don't worry. I have tools for you," Xochi said. She turned behind her and found a set of tools, which she handed to Li.

Xochi started passing around several artist's books. "These are all simple fold books. Note that the last one has some pamphlets stitched into the folds. These are what we'll be working on today. The books I'm passing around now will show you how a fold book can be very original and creative. So take a good look at each one. Then select the book style you want to make."

Li was last to receive the sample books. He chose a simple one made of one large piece of paper, very similar to one Xochi had already shown him a day earlier. The other students were muttering to themselves and to each other as they selected their books. Each student had a tool that Xochi called a "bone folder." Li decided it must be made out of some kind of bone. He followed Xochi's instructions on the proper way to score creases in the paper with the bone folder, and then fold the book properly and press the fold with the bone folder. The other students did the same although the instructions were different for each student because each one had chosen a different book model.

Li knew he would have to use the razor knife to cut an opening between the middle folds. No problem. He'd used a razor knife to fillet fish plenty of times in the restaurant kitchen where he worked. He began cutting the fold. He glanced up. Xochi was watching him, a smile on her lips.

"Li, I see you know how to use your razor," Xochi nodded. She could see that he was very familiar with razors as a cutting tool. Uh oh, he laughed to himself. Busted.

"Yes ma'am," he said. One of the girls looked at Li and giggled.

It didn't take long before each student had finished her first fold book. "Now we're going to use some book board for a cover. We can paint on it directly, or paste some decorative paper on it. Here's your pre-cut board. I pre-cut it because book board is harder to cut, and I don't want anyone to hurt themselves with their razor knife." She glanced at Li again. He ducked his head and pressed his lips together so he wouldn't laugh. "Then I'll show you how to paste your cover to the correct place on your fold book."

They continued in this manner until each student, including Li, had completed models of four different types of fold books.

"How about if we take a few minutes' break?" Xochi asked. "I can make us some coffee or I have iced water."

Li stood up and stretched. He could see that Xochi noticed that all three university students were watching him closely.

"I'm so sorry, ladies, but I have to go now," Li said. "I have to go to work soon. So I'm going to say goodbye for now. Thank you, Xochi."

The university girls groaned. "We'll miss you," one said. The look on her face could best be described at pouting.

He retrieved a business card for his restaurant from a pocket and handed it to one of the girls. "Please share this."

All three girls giggled.

Xochi nodded. "I'll follow you out." She followed Li to her apartment door and closed the door behind them. They were in the hall now.

"What's up? Are you bored?"

"No, not at all. I'm exhausted. I couldn't sleep last night worrying about you so I'm going to go take a little nap before I have to go to work. I apologize. I'm just really tired."

Xochi nodded. "I'm sorry, Li. I don't want you to lose sleep over me. I'll come and check on you when the class is over. We only have another hour or so to go." She turned to go, then she turned back to Li. She chuckled. "Very entertaining, Li. Today, I got to see Li, the ladies' man, the one Nina told me about." She laughed again and patted his cheek.

As he walked to his apartment down the hall, he heard Xochi say, "Okay, let's finish the covers and then it will be time to sew a pamphlet into your books. We have just enough time left in the class to do both."

Back in his apartment, Li fell on his bed. He hadn't been kidding about being exhausted. He'd tossed and turned all night thinking about Xochi. Yeah, sure, he was worried about Xochi's brother showing up again and trying to force her to go with him. But Li's inability to sleep was more than that. It was her. So lovely. So sweet. He wanted her. Should he make a move? She liked him. But he didn't want to come across as that ladies' man with her. He wanted her to take him seriously. Eventually he dozed off.

Li woke up about an hour and a half later. Some sound had awakened him. He realized that it was the sound of his apartment door closing. "What the hell?" he muttered to himself. He pulled himself off his bed and went into his kitchen. He immediately noticed a note on his kitchen table.

"To my favorite Ladies' Man, I miss you, you sleepy head. My class is over, and my students are gone. I'm going to run down to the market, and get us some fruit and maybe something to eat for lunch so you won't have to cook. How about a sandwich? I won't be gone long."

"*Merde!*" Li groaned as he threw open his door, ran down the hall and descended the stairs three at a time. He burst out of the front door and headed down the street toward the market, which was three blocks away. He looked for her up the street toward Fourth Avenue. There she was. Xochi was walking briskly away from the Casa Pacifica Apartments, carrying an empty shopping bag in her hand. He immediately took off after her.

Before Li could reach Xochi, her brother Manny jumped out of his car parked across the street. Her brother ran to her and stopped just short of crashing into her. By that time, Li had reached Xochi. He stood next to her, glaring at Manny, but he said nothing.

"What a nasty surprise," Xochi growled at Manny, venom in her voice. "I thought you finally woke up and realized I wasn't going with you. I'm not marrying some stranger. Never ever. But it looks like you are still suffering that delusion. So get it now! I will *never* go with you! You can go home, you *pinche* piece of shit."

Manny was staring at Li now, his face contorted with anger. "So you have your Chink pet with you," he sneered.

"Don't you call him that, you racist pig!" Xochi jumped forward and shoved Manny. He went backwards off the curb and fell down hard on his butt. He jumped up and came back with a furious move toward Xochi. He reached out for her and grabbed her arm just as he'd done at Comida Park. This time he twisted her arm just enough to hurt as he tried to jerk her toward him.

Xochi cried in pain, but she did what Li had told her to do. She moved her body forward toward her brother, putting him off balance. Li was there now. He had his hand on Manny's other arm, twisting it upward and backwards. At the same time, Li's foot crunched into the back of Manny's knee, and Manny went down to the street again. Manny glared up at him. "I have a gun, and I'm not afraid to use it. Just try touching me again," he growled.

"Stop right there!" a loud voice came from the street in front of Casa Pacifica Apartments. Tucson Police Detective Alvarez was out of his car now and moving toward them. He had a gun in his hands. It was pointed at Manny.

"Let her go," Alvarez commanded. Manny released Xochi's arm and stepped back. Alvarez had reached him now, and he said in a low, rough voice. "Turn around." Alvarez reached for his handcuffs and said, "I'm arresting you for assault."

"You can't arrest me for assault!" Manny yelled. "Arrest Xochi! She hit me first."

Alvarez frowned. He turned to Xochi and asked, "Is this true? Did you assault him first?"

Xochi grimaced. "No! He was going to grab me so I just pushed him off the curb before he could get to me. He fell down."

"Fell down? You pushed me down!" Manny said. He looked at Alvarez. "She assaulted me!"

Alvarez turned to Li. "Is that right?"

Li frowned and nodded yes. "But you remember what we told you about Manny grabbing her when we were out at the Tanque Verde Swap Meet? He assaulted her first. And you should know that he just told us he has a gun, and he threatened to use it."

"He's my brother. He's trying to force me to go across the border and marry some dumb ass *pinche* shithead that I don't even know."

"Shut up, bitch!" Manny growled.

"Okay. Enough of that," Alvarez spoke to Manny in a firm voice. "Turn around. Open your coat." There was no gun. Alvarez patted him down. Still no gun. He turned to Xochi. "I can't arrest him for simple assault if you assaulted him first, Miss Navarro. And I'm not going to arrest you because I didn't see you assault him." He shifted attention to Manny. "Let's see your passport."

Manny fished around in his pockets and pulled out his Mexican passport.

Alvarez took a good look at the passport. "Looks like you are here legally, but you are on thin ice. I think it's time for you to go back home. I'll call Border Patrol to escort you if necessary."

"Okay. Okay. Okay. I'm going." Manny turned and stomped to his car. He turned on the engine and drove away, tires screeching.

Alvarez shook his head. He turned to Xochi and Li. "More excitement at Casa Pacifica."

Li grinned. "We don't want you to get bored. Thanks, Detective Alvarez."

Alvarez nodded. "Let's go see Logan Reid. I have some news of interest for you."

They looked back to the Casa Pacific apartments. Logan Reid was standing on the front porch watching everything. As they approached, Logan smiled at Alvarez. "Come on in, Chito." He nodded at Li and Xochi. "You, too."

"Chito?" Li asked.

Logan nodded. "We're getting to know our favorite Tucson police detective."

"Yeah, everyone calls me Chito except my mom who insists on Julio." Alvarez looked a little embarrassed.

"No problem," Li said. "I have name issues myself."

They all went into Logan's apartment and found a seat.

"Where's your little bounce-on-his toes motor mouth?" Li asked.

"Zoey took him off somewhere to watch birds. They went to a dog park because they have Marc and Angela's dog Gwenny with them. I doubt they'll see many birds because those dogs get all the attention." Logan turned to Chito Alvarez. "I got your text. You have something to tell us?"

"Yeah." Alvarez turned to Xochi. "Obviously you still have a problem with your brother. You may have to get a lawyer to deal with him. Or at least get a consultation on how to deal with him." He paused and grinned. "Of course, you could always get married. If you are married, he can't demand that you marry someone else."

Xochi glanced at Li. He was smiling at her. He could see her blushing.

Alvarez pulled a notebook out of his pocket. "Due diligence here. I checked out all your students, Miss Navarro."

"Call me Xochi. Please."

Alvarez nodded. "Everyone turned out to be pretty much like what you said except for one of your students in the second class. Brian Parker."

Xochi's eyebrows went up. "What's different about Brian?"

"He's the head of a small accounting firm and a CPA. But he also has a whole other life online. He's a big cryptocurrency investor. And he has a side gig as a collector of old and valuable books. It's like a very serious hobby. He buys and sells them. I learned new words like 'antiquarian' and 'vintage' and 'rare' and 'collectible' that apply to the books he handles. He describes himself as a 'curator' and helps buyers build a collection. And he has his own collection of rare books."

Xochi was surprised. "But not artist's books?"

"No. Not unless the artist's book is old and rare and super valuable," Alvarez answered. "He never spoke to you about this interest of his?"

"No," Xochi said. "Not a word. I guess I don't know anything about this."

"Do you have any really valuable books in your apartment?" Alvarez continued.

"Just the artist's books, some of which have some value, not a whole lot, but more as art." Xochi glanced at Li.

"Xochi, remember that box you have pushed back on the high shelf in your studio closet? Remember the Chinese scroll wrapped up in leather?" Li was frowning. "Did Parker know about this?"

"I don't think so. I didn't know about the scroll myself until we opened the box."

"Wait a minute," Alvarez said. "What's this about a Chinese scroll?"

"My great-grandfather left me a box of old books. He had his own small collection, which he passed on to me. We opened the box for the first time, and Li helped me. One of the books is actually a very old Chinese scroll, and it's wrapped up in a leather sheath."

"The writing is an old form of Mandarin. There are stamps in red ink that indicate this scroll may have been created during the Ming Dynasty," Li said.

"Ming Dynasty?" Logan was surprised. "Wow. That really is old." He began searching on his smart phone. "It says here the Ming Dynasty covers the years 1368 to 1644."

"I suspect it has substantial value," Li added. "If we can learn what the text says, it may turn out to be worth a whole lot of money. We didn't open it because we didn't want to damage it. There may be paintings on the scroll as well as the calligraphy."

"And Parker didn't ask you about antique books or scrolls? And you didn't mention them?" Álvarez asked Xochi.

She shook her head 'no.' "Li put it back on the top shelf for me. I decided that I would get it out someday and try to learn more, find out if it's worth anything, and decide if I should keep it or try to sell it."

"We didn't look at the other books in the box. There may be other books that are valuable, too," Li added.

"Parker hasn't been back here, right? He hasn't contacted you about any of this?"

"No." Xochi looked worried.

Li spoke up. "Look. I have to go to work, but it looks to me like Xochi may be in danger, not only from her brother, but this guy Parker may turn out to be a problem." He turned to Xochi. "Promise me you'll stay in my apartment until I get home?"

"You can come and eat dinner with Zoey and Charlie and me," Logan smiled. "Then go to Li's apartment." He turned to Li and said, "I'll make sure she behaves." He turned and grinned at Xochi.

Li chuckled. "Good luck on that."

"Okay," Xochi said, subdued. "I get it. And I'll be good. I promise." She reached out and took Li's hand.

He squeezed her hand. "Thanks, Detective. Uh...I mean Chito. We'll get this figured out and make sure Xochi stays safe."

8 CHANGES

Li took a break from his chef job and texted Xochi a couple of times during the evening. The first time he texted her, she was still with Logan, Zoey, and Charlie in their apartment downstairs. The second time, she promised him that she was back in his apartment waiting for him. He hoped to hell she would stay there, and he told her so.

"I'll be good! I promise. Cross my heart."

"You better stay there or you'll be in big trouble."

"Stop flirting with me!"

Li could imagine her giggling. Oh my god, he groaned to himself. He decided to call her. She answered immediately.

"Hello, Handsome," Xochi giggled.

"I'm *not* flirting. I'm dead serious. You'd better stay in my apartment, or you'll be in trouble!"

"Tell me all about getting in trouble with you. Otherwise I'll have to fantasize." She giggled.

"Oh, good grief! I'm going back to work now. I'll see you in a couple of hours."

He was pleased to find Xochi sound asleep on his sofa again when he arrived home. He dropped into his bed and fell asleep fairly quickly. This time, he slept a little better knowing that her brother had gone south across the border again. He was really glad Chito Alvarez had been there to send Manny home.

The next morning when they were eating breakfast, Xochi looked at Li and grinned. "Do you know what those art students said about you when you left my studio yesterday?"

"I have no idea."

Xochi rocked her head side to side and wiggled her eyebrows. Her voice went up, and she squealed, "Oh my god. He's so *cute!*" She burst into laughter.

Li shook his head and grimaced. "Cute? I don't want to be cute."

"Well, then, what do you want to be?"

"How about devastatingly handsome? That's way better than cute." He smiled.

Xochi leaned forward and kissed him. "That's what *I* say about you. Devastatingly handsome."

"That's better." Li's smile turned into a grin.

"Hey, guess what? Logan gets his diploma this afternoon. He's earned a PhD in philosophy, and we've been invited to the graduation ceremony this afternoon."

"Oh, yeah. Thanks for the reminder. Want to go?"

"For sure!" she said.

"What do you want to do this morning?"

"Work in my studio to get ready for my next class. I heard about a new food truck not too far from here. Want to check it out and get some lunch there?"

"Absolutely! And I'll accompany you this morning to your studio."

"I have some music to play for you. Do you know any *cumbia* tunes?"

Li shook his head 'no.'

"*Cumbia* is a music genre and dance originally from Colombia. But Mexicans made it their own." She shook her head. "How did you manage to live in Tucson so long and know so little about Mexican culture?"

Li shrugged. "I was in school studying, then I went off to China for a while, then I came back here where I spent most of my time with Chinese Americans or people who dig Chinese food."

Xochi shook her head. "*Pobrecito*. I'm going to help you expand your horizons." She stood up. "Okay, let's go to my apartment, then we'll get a quickie lunch. We're meeting our Casa Pacifica pals at one this afternoon, and we'll all go together to Logan's graduation."

"And I'll call in sick."

"You're gonna get fired if you keep getting sick."

"I wish."

Xochi laughed.

"Let's go." He grabbed his guitar and followed Xochi to her apartment.

* * *

Logan sat in his favorite chair and stared out the front living room window of his apartment. He was thinking about what life was like less than a year earlier. So many changes had occurred since then. Chief among those changes was Zoey Corban. He never dreamed that he would fall in love again, or that he would propose marriage to a woman, or be so happy thinking about building a life with her and with his son Charlie. He smiled thinking about the changes.

He heard a soft knock on his door, but before he could say anything, Zoey entered. She approached him and put her arms around his shoulders. "How is my favorite man? Are you ready for your graduation ceremony?"

"I guess I'm ready. It will be kind of boring really. I just walk across the stage, and the dean will hand me my diploma. That's it."

"We'll all be so proud to see you graduate, especially Charlie."

"All? Is someone else coming?"

"All of us at Casa Pacifica. Marc and Angela and Xochi and Li and Frida."

"Frida? Is she home?"

"Yes, she came in last night. I ran into her in the laundry room. I invited her, and she said she'd be there for sure. Also I invited Chito Alvarez."

"Really? Is he coming, too?"

"He said he would be there if he could. He's working on a theft case today."

Logan nodded. "That will be fun to look out in the audience, and see all of you." He sighed. "Thank you, Zoey. You're a sweetheart. You're *my* sweetheart." He kissed her.

"Where's Charlie?"

"Taking a nap. I'll have to wake him up soon because we need to go to the auditorium for the graduation ceremony."

"What do you want to do right now?" she asked.

"Make out with you." Logan grinned.

Zoey laughed. "We're going to have a good life, Logan Reid. We'll have good food to eat, a nice place to live, a happy son, good friends, and lots of hot sex."

Logan laughed. "I like that!" He kissed her again.

Two hours later, Logan was sitting in Centennial Hall, the location of the Convocation Ceremony for his college. The Convocation was a smaller event than the much larger Commencement Ceremony for all graduating University of Arizona students. Now he was surrounded by others just like him, dressed in a graduation gown with a graduation cap on his head, the tassel off to one side. They were listening to one speaker after another. He glanced around. He could just see Zoey sitting at the end of a row on the other side of the main aisle and several rows higher in the auditorium. Charlie was next to her in his own seat. Next to Charlie were all the other Casa Pacifica residents. He noticed Chito Alvarez coming down the far isle. He sat down next to Frida. Tears come to Logan's eyes. He was sorry his parents couldn't come, but here was the Casa Pacifica gang. They were like a family. He was so grateful for them all.

The ceremony proceeded as he had predicted. Not exactly exciting. There were plenty of speeches. Then Logan found himself in a line of students, all going one-by-one up the stairs to the stage, walking toward the dean, and accepting a diploma in a leather case. Logan took his diploma and headed back to his seat. But before he could get very far, he heard Charlie.

"Daddy! Daddy!" Charlie pushed past Zoey, and he went running down the aisle. He never stopped yelling, "Daddy! Daddy!"

The audience began to titter, then full laughter exploded, followed by enthusiastic clapping. Charlie ran straight to Logan and jumped into his dad's arms. Logan was laughing now. He held Charlie for a minute then he said, "Okay, Charlie. I have to go sit with my class. Go back to Zoey, and I'll meet you when this is over. I love you."

"I love you, too, Daddy." He jumped down and returned to his seat.

After the ceremony, all the Casa Pacifica residents surrounded Logan and congratulated him. Logan gave Frida a hug and said, "When we have our Sunday potluck, we'll want to hear all about your adventures. Zoey and I will have an announcement, too."

Frida hugged him, then she went off with Marc and Angela. As they walked away, Logan heard her say, "I want to know you, Angela, and Marc, I want to meet this dog you brought home with you."

Detective Alvarez approached Logan and shook his hand. "Congratulations," Alvarez said.

"Thanks for coming. By the way, I have good news. We'll have an apartment coming open very soon. Actually, now really. It's the one bedroom downstairs, Zoey's old apartment. I'll give you the details later, but you can start moving in whenever you want. Can you come by, maybe Saturday morning, and we'll talk about the lease? Also, be sure to come to our Sunday evening potluck so you can meet everyone and catch up with the latest events and gossip."

"That's great news that an apartment is opening up so soon. I'll be there both Saturday morning and Sunday evening. And I'll start packing!" Alvarez smiled. "I'm going back to work now."

Logan waved to everyone. "I'm taking Zoey and Charlie out to eat this evening to celebrate. Tomorrow we're going on a hike and to watch birds. All three of us. So be sure to come to our Sunday potluck. We'll have lots of news for you." He turned to Zoey and Charlie. "Let's go home."

"Daddy, when we go to the restaurant, can we get some ice cream?"

"Sure. Whatever you want, Charlie. We're going to celebrate," Logan smiled.

* * *

Back in his apartment, Li sat on his sofa with Xochi sitting next to him. He reached for her hand. "I want to talk to you about something really serious."

She looked at him and nodded. "I'm listening."

"I just want to tell you that you've been an inspiration to me. You've confronted and overcome obstacles, and you dedicated yourself to the life you want to live. I've decided to try the same for me. I'm going to quit my job and start a food truck business. I know it will be a challenge and a lot of work, I won't get rich, but I think I'll be a happier person."

Xochi smiled. "You're brave."

"I want to be brave. You've helped me to look at the big picture and at least attempt to build a life for myself that satisfies me. And..," he grinned. "I'll have more time to spend with you."

"I especially like that part about us spending more time together. And if there's any way for me to help you, just let me know."

"Also, there's something else I want to say. If you think it would get your brother off your back, we could get engaged. Tell him we're going to get married. Then he'll know you're not available to him anymore. I'll make sure that he understands that you're my girl."

Xochi's eyes filled with tears. She sighed. "I'm deeply grateful for your offer. But I don't think that would work. Knowing Manny, he'd just come after you. He would try to scare you off, or eliminate you. He's dangerous. I couldn't live with myself if you got hurt or worse...," She wiped away her tears.

Li nodded. "Okay. I'll let you decide what's best for you, and I'll try to help you. As for now, I'm going to the restaurant for a little while, and I'm going to hand in my resignation. The manager will be super pissed off to get a resignation with such short notice, or no notice really. But I'm fed up. I'm ready for a change."

Xochi nodded. "I'll stay here while you're gone. I promise."

"That's a relief."

"Will you go with me to my apartment before you go? I'd like to get some of the materials I have ready to make a couple of codex books."

"Those are the ones with the pretty stitching on the book's spine?"

"That's right. That will keep me busy until you get home."

"Sure. Let's do that right now." Li started to stand up.

"Wait a minute." Xochi reached for his hand and pulled him back next to her.

"What?"

"I need a hug and a kiss, please."

Li complied. His kiss turned into more than one kiss, and they were all long and intense. He finally let her go. "You're the best thing that's ever happened to me."

"And you're the best thing that's ever happened to me." Xochi grinned and kissed him again. "I don't want to stop kissing you. But for now, let's go get my book materials."

They went down the hall to Xochi's apartment. Li sat on her sofa with a straw basket by his side. He waited while she gathered her materials, which she brought and deposited into the basket. She went into her bedroom for a few minutes, and at one point, she came into the living room and looked into the storage units where she kept her collection of artist's books. After a few minutes of this, Xochi came and sat down next to him on the sofa.

"Li," she said. Her voice was trembling.

"Is something wrong?"

"Someone has been here. Someone has been in my apartment."

Li sat up straight. Alarm filled his body. "What do you mean? What makes you think someone has been here?"

"It's little things. Subtle things. Someone has been here going through things in my studio. I found several tools and sample books moved, moved just slightly. I know where I left those things after the class yesterday. Nothing is quite the same. I looked in my bedroom, too. And here in the living room. Small things. Most people might not notice, but I noticed. Someone has been here."

Li sat quietly for a moment. He put his arm around her shoulders. "If you're right about this, then that means someone has a key to your apartment. And it appears that they are looking for something."

"But the locks were changed. Logan arranged that."

"Yes, but somehow someone got a copy of the new key."

"I don't think that was Manny."

"No, it's very unlikely that it was Manny. We had that incident on the street yesterday. Manny couldn't have gotten into your apartment before that, and Alvarez sent him packing yesterday. He's supposed to be back in Sonora now. Anyway, sneaking around doesn't seem like anything Manny would do. He's not exactly the subtle type to acquire a key secretly and come in while you're gone. He's a confrontational type of guy. It has to be someone else."

"I don't know what to do."

"We're going to talk to Logan and to Detective Alvarez, and get their opinion. We can't do it tonight because Logan said he's going out to dinner with Zoey and Charlie. I'll text him and ask for a morning meeting with him and Alvarez."

Xochi nodded. "Okay. That's a good idea."

"Let's go back to my apartment with your book materials. I don't like leaving you even for a little while, but it can't be helped."

"I promise I'll stay put in your apartment."

They returned to Li's apartment. Xochi took over a small table and sat up a lamp. She began working on her stitching.

Three hours later, Li returned. He unlocked his door and found Xochi on his sofa hugging a pillow.

"Hey." He grinned. "I quit my job!" He looked at Xochi. She had an odd look on her face.

"Xochi, what's going on? Did someone try to break in here?"

"No. It's been quiet here."

"Well, something happened. Tell me."

"My cousin called me. I mean the cousin who lives on my dad's old ranch in Sonora."

"Yes?"

"My cousin said that Manny and his men got into a shootout with some cartel gang members. They were at a little town called Agua Zarca south of Nogales. Manny got shot. My brother is dead."

9 A SEARCH

Li put his arm around Xochi and held her close to him.

She cried softly. "I don't know why I'm crying. I didn't really love Manny. I didn't even like him. I never spent any time with him. That fact that he was my brother didn't really mean anything to me."

"Maybe you're just sad about a life lost for no reason. Those cartel members shoot and kill a lot of people," Li said.

"Yes, I think you're right. It's just sad. They push the drugs north, and some greedy Americans smuggle the guns south across the border. So much violence." Xochi wiped her face with a tissue. She'd stopped crying now. "But enough about me. So you quit your job?"

"Yes, I was going to hand in a resignation letter. Be polite. But the manager started into one of his rants again. I just couldn't take it anymore. So I yelled back at him, and I did that in front of the other staff, which is a real no-no. That really pissed him off. He kept on yelling at me. I guess he thought I'd back down. I ended up smashing a big knife into one of the wooden cutting boards. Then I yelled back, 'I quit!' and I walked out. As I was walking out, the other staff members applauded me." Li laughed. "It was quite a scene. The manager has already texted me with a halfway apology. He wants me to come back to work, but I'm ignoring his texts."

"I'm proud of you. You are following your own path now. You'll be happier."

"I'll be happier if you just sit with me, and let me hold you."

Xochi settled against him again, cuddling really. He continued to hold her close. After a while, he realized that she'd fallen asleep. He rose, helped her to stretch out on the sofa, and covered her with a blanket. He turned off the lights, and went to his own bed. He fell sleep quickly.

The next morning as he was making coffee, Li texted Logan.

"We have some news. Xochi thinks someone has been in her apartment again. Maybe a lock problem? Could we see you before you go hiking?"

"Sure. Come now," Logan answered. "Chito Alvarez just arrived. You can tell him, too."

Li handed Xochi a cup of coffee just as she emerged from the bathroom. "Let's take our coffee with us. Logan said Detective Alvarez just arrived so we can tell them both about a possible intruder."

Five minutes later, all four were sitting at Logan's dining room table.

"Where's Charlie?" Li asked.

"Zoey and Charlie are taking Gwenny the greyhound for a quick morning walk," Logan said. "So we have a few minutes of calm." He gestured to Alvarez. "Chito is here to go over his lease. He'll be moving in soon."

"Actually I've already started moving some of my stuff in," Chito smiled.

Logan nodded. "We're in the process of helping Zoey move her things in with us, and that's making way for Chito in her old apartment. Or I should say, Chito and his new apartment."

Li smiled. "So Zoey is going to live with you and Charlie?"

Logan nodded. "We'll tell you all about it at the potluck Sunday evening."

"Logan, let's start with these two since they're here now." Alvarez gestured to Xochi and Li. "The lease business won't take much time."

Logan nodded his agreement. "Sure."

"What's this about someone in your apartment?" Alvarez asked.

"We didn't actually see anyone," Li said. "But Xochi is quite sure someone was there." He looked at Xochi. "Want to explain?"

Xochi took a deep breath. "I found a number of items very slightly disturbed," she started. "My tools weren't quite where I'd left them. I mean they were there but just not in the same exact place. I saw several drawers in chests that had been opened and weren't quite closed. There were big rolls of different kinds of paper that weren't in exactly the same place that I'd left them. Just subtle things."

"This doesn't sound like the first time someone broke into your place," Alvarez said.

"Not at all," Xochi agreed. "The first person totally trashed everything and made a big mess. The latest intruder was very careful. Trying not to be noticed, I'd say."

"This is definitely a problem. I contacted the real estate company after that first break-in, and they had a locksmith come in and change the locks to Xochi's door," Logan said.

"That means someone in addition to Xochi has access to the new key," Li added. "And it appears that the intruder is looking for something."

"What about that box of old books you told me about?" Alvarez asked. "The one with the Chinese scroll?"

"It wasn't disturbed at all," Xochi said. "It's hard to even see the box because it's on a high shelf. You have to be tall enough to see any part of the box. Also getting to it, much less seeing it, is even more difficult now. I put a very long roll of paper standing upright inside the closet. It's kind of in the way."

"So we don't know what exactly he's looking for. And we don't know exactly how much he knows about what you have there. Any idea how he might have come to the conclusion that you have something of value in your apartment?" Alvarez continued.

"I don't know, Detective...uh...I mean Chito. I haven't really talked to anyone about that box of books except Li," Xochi said. "We looked into the box only one time, and Li discovered the Chinese scroll there."

Logan spoke up. "Is there some way that a person might be able to hear what Xochi and Li were talking about. We discovered recently that video cameras can be installed without easily being detected."

Chito Alvarez nodded. "Yes, video cameras are a possibility, and also there are listening devices that will pick up and record conversations, and often transmit the recording. I can do a sweep of your apartment, Xochi. Want to try that?"

Xochi looked at Li. "What do you think? Do you think I'm being irrational and causing a lot of trouble?"

"No! I think we're lucky to have Chito Alvarez here. He has professional skills, and he's offering to investigate. So I say go for it."

Xochi turned to Alvarez. "Thank you. Yes, please. Go ahead and do the sweep. Maybe then we'll find out what this intruder knows and learn what he's looking for."

Alvarez nodded. "Okay. I need to go down to my car and get a detector. I'll be back in a minute." He left Logan's apartment and returned five minutes later.

"This is called an RF detector. RF stands for radio frequency." Alvarez held in his hand a small device. "It's used to find hidden surveillance equipment like video and audio devices. It's not perfect, but it actually does quite a good job most of the time. Let's go upstairs, and I'll get a search started."

All four of them went up the stairs to Xochi's apartment. Logan, Li, and Xochi watched Alvarez as he walked from room to room. He started in Xochi's living room. Nothing. He went to her bedroom next. Nothing. Then he went to her studio. Almost immediately, Alvarez got an alert from the RF detector. He looked around until he found the surveillance equipment, which was hidden under her large studio work table. He disengaged it and held it up.

"Looks like an audio recording device. This is one that transmits the audio via wi-fi to another device such as a computer or Android phone. We can listen to the recording and learn what was sent."

"I think I know what was recorded and sent," Li said. "Xochi and I had a conversation in this room about artist's books. During this same afternoon, we retrieved the box and found the Chinese scroll. We talked about that, too."

Xochi nodded. "That's right. I also taught a book arts class here, but the book box and Chinese scroll was not mentioned at all in the class. The key conversation here was between me and Li, and it was about the box of old books and the scroll."

"Since your place was broken into earlier and there was so much damage done, I think this will be another component of Tucson Police Department's already on-going investigation. I'm going to take this in and have one of our techs find out what's been recorded, and possibly make a print out of the conversation, plus the time and day it took place. If that comes out as we expect, then we can assume that the perpetrator knows you have this box of books, and he's looking for it. He hasn't found it so that means he'll be back." He turned to Li. "Xochi can stay with you? I think it's best that she not stay in her apartment, especially if she's alone."

Li nodded. "She's staying with me. She's sleeping on my sofa."

Logan spoke up. "And I'm going to try to find out how it is that this intruder got a key to Xochi's apartment."

Alvarez looked at Xochi and Li. "I'm sorry, but I need to get going. I want to move some more boxes into my new apartment now because I have to go to work this afternoon. I'll get back to you about what's on the recording." He turned to Logan. "Can we take a quick look at that lease and I'll sign it now?"

"Sure. So let's get together later and discuss all this. Okay? Meanwhile, you two be careful," Logan said.

"We will," Li said.

* * *

Xochi and Li went back to his apartment.

"I'll make us some breakfast," Li said.

"I'm going to my apartment just to get some clean clothes. I want to take a shower here if that's okay."

"Yes, that's fine with me. But I'll go with you now."

"That's not necessary. I'll only be gone five minutes. Anyway, I seriously doubt the intruder will come in here during the day."

Li frowned. "I'll leave my door open, and you call me if you have a problem."

"Yes, sir!" she giggled.

"You're such smart ass." He headed for his kitchen. He noticed immediately that Xochi had closed his apartment door. He opened it, and he returned to the kitchen.

Li was breaking eggs into a bowl when he heard the noise. Or just a sound. Like a cry. He stopped and went to his open door. There it was again. This time, he recognized Xochi's voice. She was crying out, "Stop! Leave me alone!" He immediately ran down the hall, threw open the door to Xochi's apartment and charged in.

A man Li had never seen before had Xochi pinned to her sofa. He was tearing at her clothing, and Li could see that the man had already ripped open her blouse. She was struggling against him and yelling, but she was too small to fight him off. He wasn't a big man, but he was big enough and strong enough to overcome her. Now he was pulling at her pants. Li could see her pants had an elastic waist, and it was going to be easy for him to get the pants ripped down off her hips. The bastard was going to rape Xochi! Li felt total fury wash over him. Then he heard the man say, "Come on, baby. You want it. You know you want it." That was all it took.

Li yelled, "Stop! Get your hands off her!" as he charged forward.

This startled the intruder. He stopped just long enough for Xochi to free her arms and hands. She punched the man in the face and screamed, "Get off me, you piece of shit!"

By this time, Li had crossed the room. He grabbed the man at the back of his neck and one shoulder, and shoved him to the center of the room. Before the man could react, Li tightened his grip on the man's arm and twisted it backwards with a violent thrust. The arm separated from the shoulder socket, and the man screamed in pain. Li wasn't finished. He took the now dislocated arm and twisted it again. With a sharp blow, Li smashed his fist into the humerus, the upper arm bone. The bone cracked, and the man screamed again. Li threw the man to the floor, and he ran to Xochi.

"Oh, Li. I'm so sorry. I should have stayed with you."

"You are such a pain in the butt, Xochi. You should listen to me. Are you okay?"

"Yeah, I'm sorry." She put her arms around Li.

"Who is this asshole?"

"My student. Brian Parker."

Parker had struggled to his feet now. "You two are going to be really sorry by the time I get through with you. Xochi, where is that box with the Chinese scroll?"

"I'm not going to tell you!" she shouted.

"Why are you so interested in the Chinese scroll? You collect old books? Or Chinese scrolls? Or what?" Li demanded.

"I collect money," Parker growled. "That scroll is worth over a million dollars. Your great-grandfather outbid me for it. When he died, I figured either your mom or you inherited it. I want it! Now!" He reached to his back with his one still-functioning arm and hand, and he pulled out a very small handgun from a back pocket.

"So you think you can get away with the scroll, and you think we won't report you?" Li asked in a calm voice. He could see a movement by the door. Detective Alvarez. Parker had his back to the door and didn't know Alvarez was there.

"You two won't be around long enough to report me. My little pistol shoots real bullets, and those bullets will take you out."

"Drop the gun!" Alvarez shouted. He had taken the classic law enforcement stance, feet apart, arms extended, both hands on his Glock 22 service gun.

Parker turned toward Alvarez, but instead of dropping his pistol, he lifted his arm and pointed it at Alvarez.

Detective Alvarez took one shot. Parker fell to the floor again, screaming in pain.

Li jumped forward and kicked Parker's gun out of reach.

Alvarez was already on his phone, calling for reinforcements and an ambulance. He went to Parker and pulled the man into a sitting position. "Sit quietly and don't move, or I'll ask Li here to dislocate your other arm." Parker remained still, groaning in pain.

Alvarez turned to Xochi. "So this is your former student? The one we discussed earlier?"

"Yes," Xochi said. "He told us that the Chinese scroll is worth over a million dollars."

"And he threatened to kill us with his gun," Li added.

"Yeah, I heard that," Alvarez responded. "That's a .25 Automatic Colt Pistol. First time I've ever seen one. Tiny little things, but potentially very deadly."

Within five minutes, a cop car arrived, sirens blaring and lights flashing. The ambulance wasn't far behind.

By now, Logan was standing at the door of Xochi's apartment. "What the hell is going on?"

Alvarez looked at him and grinned. "More excitement at Casa Pacifica apartments."

Logan groaned and shook his head.

Two police officers entered Xochi's apartment. They were followed by the ambulance paramedics and a gurney. Parker was formally arrested and taken off to the nearest hospital emergency room.

"Detective...Chito...you know the backstory here. So can I take Xochi back to my apartment? She's very upset. I want to see if I can help her calm down." Xochi was sobbing now.

"Yeah, sure. I'll catch up with you later." Alvarez looked at Logan, a grin on his face. "I'm going to like living here."

Logan groaned again. "I hope you can bring some peace and quiet to this place."

"I'll do my best. Okay. I'm off again. I have to finish moving those boxes into my new apartment. And I have a case I'm working on. A different case, I mean. So I'm outta here for now. I'll see you at the potluck tomorrow evening."

"Thanks, Chito," Logan said.

Li turned to Logan. "We're going to seek some of that peace and quiet now."

"Good idea. I'm totally in favor of peace and quiet." Logan turned and went back to his apartment to wait for Zoey, his talkative little boy Charlie, and an enthusiastic dog that like to play ball with Charlie in their living room. "Yeah, peace and quiet," he muttered to himself.

Li took Xochi's hand. "Come with me. I'll fix you breakfast, and we'll eat. And let's try to relax."

"I'm sorry, Li. I shouldn't have gone to my apartment alone. I should have listened to you."

"Yes, you should have listened to me. But I forgive you." He chuckled.

They were back in his apartment now.

Xochi turned to Li and put her arms around him. She held him close, and he pulled her even closer.

She looked up at him. "It's time for me to declare myself."

Li kissed her. "What do you mean?"

"You know that beautiful song you played for me? *Clouds*? I looked up the lyrics in English. One phrase says, *"So my light heart would darken too, If I ever lost you."* That says it all. That's how I feel. I'm crazy about you. You are everything I've always looked for in a man. You are sweet and funny, and devastatingly handsome, and you take care of me, and you are sexy as hell. I love you, Li. I love you so much."

Li nodded. "I love you, too. You're a lot of trouble, but I think maybe I'll be able to rein you in."

"Well, I don't know about that." She giggled. "But I'll try to start directing my energy away from causing trouble and toward helping you. If you want to open a food truck business, I'm going to help you. Whatever you want, I am going to do my best to help you get it."

"All I want right now is you."

"I can help you with that." She took Li's hand and led him to his bedroom.

10 ANOTHER POTLUCK

Li stood in his kitchen and stared at the stove. He was thinking about the Sunday potluck dinner for all the residents of Casa Pacifica Apartments. But he did not want to make *jiaozi* again for the potluck. He didn't want to cook anything at all. Maybe he could just put some cut-up veggies, cheese, and crackers on a plate, and go with that. He sighed and smiled. All he wanted to do was think about last night, the night he'd spent with Xochi, probably the best night of his life. Before they went to sleep after hours of love-making, she whispered to him, "*Wǒ ài nǐ*, I love you." And he loved her, too. He told her so.

They slept late. Then they ate a late brunch at a food truck that was new to Li. They came home and spent the afternoon in bed again enjoying each other. Xochi woke up all energetic, told him she was going shopping, and he should play his guitar while she was gone. He wanted to go with her, but she reminded him that Manny was gone, Parker was in police custody, and the chance of her being assaulted on the street or at the market was very unlikely. He agreed. She was much safer now, and he knew he couldn't be with her every minute.

But play his guitar? Li felt so lazy that he didn't even do that. He did nothing. His neighbor Marc had taught him that great Italian phrase, *Il dolce far niente*. The sweetness of doing nothing. Yeah, that was what Li was doing today. Nothing. Sweet nothing.

He looked down at his feet. Bonita the cat was rubbing against his legs, purring and occasionally meowing. "Are you hungry, Bonita? Don't worry. I'll feed you." He found her bowl and filled it with dry cat foot, then he added some chicken broth and a bit of shredded chicken. The cat approved and began eating enthusiastically.

"Li, I'm home!" Xochi came into his apartment. She was carrying a big bag from the local market a short distance up their street. She looked at him and shook her head. "You're supposed to be playing your guitar. You're not thinking of cooking, are you?"

"I don't really feel like cooking," Li answered.

"Then don't cook. I'm making dinner to take to the potluck. You get a pass this week."

"You're going to cook? Wow! It's really past time to get started cooking. What are you going to make?"

"Soup. Chicken noodle soup with carrots and celery."

"That's pretty complicated for an artist who doesn't like to cook." Li wiggled his eyebrows. "Want me to help?"

"No. I can manage. Bring out a big pot, and I'll get started. You can watch." She was grinning at him. "Of course, you could make things easier on me if you took off all your clothes. I need the inspiration."

"What?!" He was laughing now. "We'll never make it to the potluck if I take off my clothes because then you'd have to take off your clothes and one thing would lead to another and..."

"Okay. I get it. Leave your clothes on. Be boring, if you insist. Where's that big pot that I need?"

Li found the pot, put it on the stove, and stood back. His eyes went wide as he watched her pull twelve cans of soup out of the grocery bag, open them, and pour the contents into the pot. The twelve cans were all the same brand of chicken noodle soup featuring carrots and celery. He began to laugh.

"Canned soup?" he guffawed. "Seriously?"

"It's good soup!" She sniffed. "Don't be such an elitist!"

"Oh, my god." Li couldn't stop laughing.

"Just don't tell anyone." Xochi winked at him.

He snickered. "I wouldn't think of it."

Twenty minutes later when the canned soup had heated up, they headed down to Logan's apartment.

Everyone was there. Logan, Zoey, Charlie, Marc, Angela, and Frida. They were all sitting around drinking wine, gossiping and laughing, everyone except for Charlie who was chasing a ball across the floor with Gwenny. Her tail wagged constantly, and Charlie giggled constantly, too.

"Hi, Li. Hi, Xochi. Glad you made it. Put your pot there in the kitchen," Logan said.

"Hey, you two. Great to see you again," Frida called out. "Logan, where's that cute guy I met briefly at your graduation? Is he coming?" she asked.

"Cute guy?" Logan grinned. "You must mean Chito." He wondered how Frida would react when she found out that Chito Alvarez was a cop. What would Frida, the labor union organizer who had been arrested several times at union demonstrations, think? "Don't worry. He'll be here." And what would Chito think about Frida?

Just at that moment, there was a knock at the door. Charlie ran to the door and threw it open.

"Hi!" he said loudly. "Are you Mr. Alvarez?"

"Yes, sir," Chito Alvarez said with a grin. "And this is my daughter Isabel."

Isabel, a very pretty little girl about Charlie's size and age, leaned up against her dad. She smiled shyly.

Charlie grinned. "Hi, Isabel. I'm Charlie. I'm almost six years old. Come on and I'll introduce you to Gwenny." The two children quickly found the greyhound drinking from her water bowl in the kitchen. Gwenny followed them into the living room, and the three began to roll the ball around on the floor.

Logan stood. "Okay. I think we all know each other except Frida and Chito haven't formally met." He waved his hand between the two. "Consider yourself introduced. Chito Alvarez and Frida Villarreal. And you have a daughter, Chito?"

"Yes. This is Isabel. She lives with her mom most of the time. Her mom and I split up when she was two. Her mom remarried and has two more children. I get to spend time with Isabel on any weekend days that I have free. Most of the time, though, she's with her other family. She won't be living with me here, just staying sometimes."

Logan nodded. "That's good to have another child here. Then Charlie won't be the only kid all the time." He gestured to the large dining table. "Everybody, please bring your wine, and put your dishes on the table. We'll eat first and talk later."

They followed Logan's directions. Marc and Li sat down first. They had no dishes to share. "Angela is cooking for us," Marc explained.

"And Xochi is taking her turn," Li said. He couldn't bring himself to say that Xochi had actually *cooked* anything.

Chito Alvarez put a cast iron skillet on the table. "This is a cheese and corn soufflé with peppers, but not hot peppers. My mom made it for us when I was growing up," he explained.

"Yummy," Frida said.

Xochi began transferring cups of her heated canned soup into individual bowls. Dishes were passed around, and everyone got a portion of everything. There was just enough for everyone to get about a cup of Xochi's soup, plus a little left over. Compliments from everyone abounded for all the dishes, including Xochi's soup.

"Great soup!" Frida said to Xochi. "Did our master chef Li teach you how to make it?"

Li choked and coughed. His eyes filled with tears, caused by the need to cough more, and from the ridiculous idea that he might have made that canned soup. He tried his best not to break out laughing.

"Nah," Xochi said, "his recipes are too complicated for me. I followed some easier directions."

Li looked over at her. She was grinning at him. Devil woman. He ducked his head and bit his lip to stop the urge to guffaw.

Because they were all primarily focused on the food, it didn't take long for everyone to be satisfied. While Zoey and Angela cleared the table, Logan brought out small bowls, and served everyone some ice cream.

"It's pistachio," Charlie whispered to Isabel. "Do you like pistachio?"

"Yes," she returned his whisper. "Pistachio is good. I like all kinds of ice cream. I like your dog, too."

Charlie nodded. "Gwenny is the best dog in the world."

After eating and clearing away the dishes, everyone settled on the sofa and stuffed chairs.

Logan spoke first. "Let's have announcements first. I have a very big, very happy announcement. Zoey has agreed to marry me. She's going to be my wife, and she's going to be Charlie's mom."

Everyone cheered except Zoey who broke into tears and laughed at the same time. She thrust out her hand and showed everyone her new ring. "And look at my engagement necklace! Charlie made it for me."

"Congratulations!" everyone cried. "Beautiful ring! Beautiful necklace."

Angela and Xochi exchanged grins.

"Charlie, what are you going to call Zoey now? Zoey or Mom or Mother?" Angela asked.

"Daddy called her 'sweet pea.' Am I supposed to call her that?" Charlie looked confused.

"I want you to call me Mom," Zoey said. She hugged Charlie. "Please call me Mom."

"Okay," Charlie said, relieved. "Isabel, let's go to my room, and we can read Gwenny a picture book. She likes it when I read to her 'cause she can't read."

The two children and Gwenny ran off to Charlie's room to read to the dog. Isabel and Charlie agreed to help each other with the words because they were both just learning to read.

Logan handed Zoey a tissue. She leaned up against him, and he kissed her. "You are all invited to the wedding," he said. "We haven't set the date yet."

Marc grinned. "Also, Logan, I remembering attending a graduation ceremony recently where you earned your PhD."

"Dr. Reid, I approve. Congratulations! Now I'm not the only doctor in the building," said Dr. Angela Brooks, everyone's favorite veterinarian. "Also I want to add that my job as a vet is wonderful. And Marc has a new exhibit of his art photos coming up. I hope everyone can attend the opening."

Murmurs of approval were voiced.

Xochi turned to Li and whispered, "Tell them about the food truck."

Li sighed. "This may be premature, but I'm seriously considering opening a food truck business. I quit my job as a chef because I needed a change. Xochi is helping me."

"Let us know when, and we'll eat at your new food truck," Logan said.

Frida spoke up, "I'm home now. I was attending a really terrific organizing workshop offered by the AFL-CIO. I'll be telling you stories about my work from time to time. I think I'll be a better union organizer now because of the workshop. And I'm hoping I won't get arrested anymore."

"Arrested?" Chito Alvarez spoke up. He looked alarmed.

"Yeah, I've been arrested five times for disturbing the peace. Getting arrested is no fun." Frida grinned. "What do you do, Chito Alvarez?"

"I'm a cop."

Frida's mouth dropped open. "A cop!"

Everyone laughed.

"Actually, Chito is a detective with the Tucson Police Department. He's really a good guy, and he's helped us a lot here at Casa Pacifica. Most recently, yesterday to be exact, he stopped a potential killer," Logan said. He turned to Xochi. "I guess we're ready to talk about that now. Want to explain what happened, Xochi?"

Xochi sighed. "I've had some real trouble lately. Li helped me more than I can express. I'm very grateful to him." She turned and squeezed Li's hand. "Here's the story. My great-grandfather left me a box of old books when he died. Li and I found a very old Chinese scroll in the box. One of my former book arts students, Brian Parker, tried to steal it. When I caught him in my apartment, Parker tried to rape me, but Li stopped him. Chito came and shot him when he was going to shoot us, and then Chito arrested him. And a few days before that, both Li and Chito helped me with my brother who was trying to force me to go back to Sonora and get married to some stranger."

"Whoa!" Frida said. "That's quite a story!"

"Seriously," said Angela. "I had no idea all this was going on!"

"I'll fill in some of the gaps," Chito said. "You all remember when Xochi's apartment was broken into and trashed? We think the intruder picked both the back-door lock and Xochi's door. Turns out that the guy who broke in is the nephew of Brian Parker, the man Xochi just mentioned. The two of them, nephew and uncle, had an agreement. The nephew was supposed to steal the scroll, Parker would sell it, and the nephew would get a cut. But the nephew couldn't find it, not to mention trashing Xochi's place in the process. The nephew's name is Ethan Parker."

Logan spoke up. "I contacted the real estate company that handles several apartment buildings, including this one. I'm the local manager only for Casa Pacifica. The real estate folks contacted their locksmith, the man who came later to change the lock on Xochi's apartment after the break-in. He admitted under pressure that he had been coerced by a man who was married to the locksmith's daughter. The man demanded a key to Xochi's apartment in exchange for promising to not beat the locksmith's daughter anymore. The locksmith wanted his daughter to be safe so he gave the key to his daughter's husband. The husband's name is Ethan Parker. After getting the key from the locksmith, Ethan Parker gave the key to Brian Parker, his uncle, thinking he'd still get a cut of the sale."

Chito took over the story. "This meant that the apartment was easy to enter with the new key. But Brian Parker decided his nephew was useless so he entered Xochi's apartment himself and installed a digital listening device. That's how he discovered where the box with the Chinese scroll was hidden. He listened to Xochi and Li's conversation about the scroll."

Xochi sighed. "Despite warnings from Li, stubborn me went by myself to my apartment, thinking I'd be there just a few minutes. But Brian Parker was there already looking for the scroll. He decided he wanted more than the scroll. He assaulted me, and when Li heard me call for help, he came and stopped Parker. He did that Chinese martial arts thing and dislocated Parker's shoulder."

"And broke his arm," Chito added. "Then Parker threatened to shoot and kill them both. I happened to be moving my boxes into my new apartment when I heard all the ruckus. I went upstairs, and I saw Parker threaten Li and Xochi with his pistol. Then he turned the pistol on me with a clear intention to shoot. I was forced to shoot him first." Chito shrugged his shoulders. "Parker is recuperating in the hospital now. When he's better, he'll be moved to the Pima County Detention Center."

"Jail, in other words," Logan added. "The locksmith was arrested, too, but he'll probably only have to pay a big fine, probation and maybe community service."

"We arrested Ethan Parker, too. Once we got his fingerprints, we were able to ID him as the one who broke into Xochi's apartment and tore everything up. He's in the Detention Center now," Chito added.

Logan looked around at all the Casa Pacifica residents. They seemed stunned. "Quite a story, huh? I'm hoping that things settle down now. And I'm really glad that Chito will be joining us."

Everyone nodded their agreement.

"Welcome, Chito. And thank you." Frida grinned.

"Just doing my job. Thanks to you all." He lowered his gaze. To Logan, he definitely appeared to be embarrassed.

"Anymore stories?" Logan asked. No response.

"Then I'll do the dishes," Marc said.

Angela looked at him and smiled. "You're so sexy."

Marc looked around, grinning. "You dudes hear that? Wanna get a girl all turned on? Offer to do the dishes."

Everyone laughed.

Xochi turned to Li. "I'll get your pot, and let's go back to your apartment. I want to talk to you about something."

"Okay." Li stood. "Goodnight, all. Have a great week." Xochi joined him with the pot in hand, and she waved goodbye to everyone.

Back in his apartment, Li and Xochi sat together on his sofa. She held his hand.

"I have some serious things to say to you." Li noticed she was frowning. Uh oh, he thought to himself.

"I love you. I love you a thousand times." She looked at him with tears in her eyes.

Li sighed with relief. "I love you, too."

Xochi sighed. "First thing. I'm going to get some help and find out how to sell off that scroll. I hope that's true that it's worth a million dollars. And you are going to get half the money."

"Oh, no. You don't need to do that. Your great-grandfather left you that. It's yours."

"Think of it this way. You rescued me from being raped and murdered by that *pendejo* Parker. And before that, you stopped my brother Manny from forcing me to go across the border with him and marry some stranger. You've been a real hero, Li. My hero. On top of that, you are so sweet, and funny, and calm and patient with me, and, oh my god, so sexy. You are an incredibly good lover. So to share that million dollars with you is no big deal compared to what you've done for me...and to me." She giggled.

"You think I'm a good lover?"

"The best lover. The best in the world."

Li grinned. "Worth a million dollars?"

"Worth a lot more than that. And don't forget that part about rescuing me." She kissed him. "And you play music for me."

He returned her kisses.

"So, here's what's going to happen," Xochi continued. "We'll get started on investigating food trucks. You can rent one and try it out, and if you like the experience, we'll get you a really nice, new food truck. I'll help you along the way with figuring out stuff like which business licenses you have to get, and hiring anyone to help you. All that money means pressure will be off me, too. I can devote myself to my art and not worry about running out of money. We'll have fun together."

"I like the sound of all this."

"Speaking of sounds, I really hope you'll play your guitar more. You're a good musician now, but you could be a really great one."

"I love to play my guitar." By now, Li was feeling warm all over, happy. No worries.

"There's something else that I may be able to help you with."

"What's that?"

"We can do a Zoom call with your parents. Do they know how to do that?"

"My parents are Chinese. They prefer WeChat."

"Okay. We'll call them together using WeChat. We'll tell them that you and I are madly in love, and we want to get married. We'll tell them that we're engaged."

"Oh, boy. They'll be upset."

"They'll get over it. I'll charm them."

He smiled. "You can be very charming, and yes, we can tell them we're engaged. Give it a try. But will we really be engaged?"

Xochi looked at him and winked. "Let's do like Angela and Marc are doing. She said that they are going with the flow. We'll tell your parents we're engaged. Then we'll go with the flow. Who knows? Maybe someday we'll really and truly want to get married. And we will."

Li nodded and smiled. "Go with the flow."

"Okay. Last thing?"

"You are so organized. What's the last thing?"

"I paint sometimes, usually highly realistic oil paintings of people. Not portraits but full figure paintings. I want you to pose for me because I want you to be the subject of my painting."

Li shrugged. "Okay. I can do that."

"Naked."

"Naked? You want me to pose naked? A naked painting of me? I don't know about that." He grimaced. How embarrassing.

Xochi sat back and relaxed. "Don't worry. I have ways to convince you. And we have plenty of time."

"You are a devil, Xochi Navarro. A devil woman." Li kissed her. "I love you anyway."

Thank you and some Information Sources:

Hello Reader!

Thank you for reading *Clouds*, the fourth Iron Horse Mystery. Please leave a review of this book wherever you buy books (Amazon, Kobo, Nook, Apple, etc.) and also at Bookbub and Goodreads. By leaving a review for others to read, you can make it much easier for mystery readers everywhere to find this book. Thank you so much. Please sign up for my monthly newsletter all about art, books, and the natural world at www.cjshane.com/contactnewsletter.html

Here is a link to Django Reinhart and his tune *Nuages (Clouds)*:
https://www.youtube.com/watch?v=DY0FF4iR9Cw

ARTIST'S BOOKS

Xochi Navarro, one of the two main protagonists in *Clouds*, is a book artist. She makes artist's books (sometimes printed without the apostrophe as "artists books"). But what is an artist's book?

The Smithsonian Libraries and Archives website blog defines artist's book this way:

"The simple answer to someone not familiar with artists' books might be: art in book form. But they are not quite so simple...An artist's book is a medium of artistic expression that uses the form or function of "book" as inspiration. It is the artistic initiative seen in the illustration, choice of materials, creation process, layout and design that makes it an art object...."

The easiest way to understand the artistic nature of an artist's book, as well as the very diverse forms an artist's book can take, is to look at multiple websites with photos of artist's books.

Look for artists books on the Smithsonian Institution website just mentioned. Another good source of information is the Center for Book Arts in New York City. Also you can go to the websites of artists who make artist's books or to universities that have collections of artist's books.

An easy way to see many photos of artist's books is to look for these books about books as an art form. Here are a few:

1000 Artists' Books: Exploring the Book as Art. Sandra Salamony and Peter & Donna Thomas, Quarry Books

500 Handmade Books, v. 1 and v.2. Lark Books

Masters: Book Arts curated by Eileen Wallace. Eileen Wallace, Lark Books

The Penland Book of Handmade Books. Lark Books

You'd be surprised at how many famous artists have made artist's books. Examples are Marc Chagall, Salvador Dali, Henri Matisse, and Pablo Picasso. Today some well-known book artists include Julie Chen.

Interested in trying your hand at making an artist's book? There are several how-to books that are great to get you started on making an artist's book. Two of my favorites are:

Cover to Cover by Shereen La Plantz

Making Handmade Books by Alisa Golden

Iron Horse Next in Series? A Closer Look

1 AN ACCIDENTAL MEETING

Logan Reid woke up suddenly, his body tense. He could hear the sound of gunshots not far away. Too close for comfort. Too close to the apartments that he managed, Casa Pacifica. "Shit," he muttered to himself. His wife, Zoey, was curled up against him, still asleep. Logan carefully edged himself away from her, rose to his feet, and quickly pulled on a t-shirt and jeans. He went into his living room, closing the bedroom door behind him.

He looked out of the big front window of his apartment, where he immediately saw a young man staggering in the street, a gun in his hand. The man clumsily lifted his arm into the air and shot the gun again. Logan heard another sound, this time coming from the hallway. Chito. He could hear Chito Alvarez, a detective with the Tucson Police Department, leaving his apartment and heading toward the front door of the building.

Logan opened his door just as Chito passed him.

"Call 911, Logan," Chito said. "Tell them I'm here and that I told you to call."

Logan nodded, returned to his apartment, found his phone and did as Chito instructed. He followed Chito out of the building into the front yard.

"Drop the gun!" Chito shouted at the young man. Logan could see that, despite being shirtless and wearing only pajama bottoms, Chito was standing with his legs apart and with both hands on his service gun, now pointed at the young man. He was a cop ready to shoot.

The young man began singing, struggling to stay on his feet. To Logan, he looked drunk or stoned or both.

"*Ain't no sunshine when she's gone,*" the young man sobbed.

"Chito, I know him," Logan said in a low voice. "He's a former student of mine. Let me try talking to him."

Chito shook his head. "This is dangerous, Logan."

"I called like you said. The cops are on their way," Logan answered. He stepped to Chito's side. "Darren, remember me? You were in my introductory philosophy class."

The young man focused on Logan. "Oh, yeah, Mr. Reid. I liked your class." He began singing again. "*Ain't no sunshine when she's gon*e."

"I have a song for you, Darren. But you have to put the gun down first."

"I like songs." He staggered forward. "Mr. Reid, my girl dumped me."

"Put the gun down, and I'll sing you a tune."

The young man, Darren, leaned forward, almost lost his balance, but he was able to place the gun onto the street pavement.

Chito moved quickly to take possession of the gun.

"Okay, here we go," Logan said. "I can't sing for shit so be patient. One of the lyrics is something like 'you don't have a girl to make you smile,' and every verse ends with this." And Logan took a deep breath and sang, "*Don't worry. Be happy.*"

"I can't be happy, Mr. Reid." Darren sobbed again. "She's gone."

"Darren, we all have our struggles. Do you remember meeting my wife Caroline?"

Darren nodded. "She was sweet to me."

"She died several years ago."

"Oh! That's so sad." Darren began crying again.

Logan stepped forward and hugged the young man. "I survived. My life now is good. You'll survive, and you'll find another girl to love." He could hear the cops coming, sirens on.

Chito stepped forward. "Darren, looks like you've had too much to drink. Or did you take some drugs?"

"I don't know. My friend gave me a pill, and he said to wash it down with the tequila."

"What was the pill?" Chito asked.

"I don't know." He turned to Logan. "Do you think I'll ever find a girl who will love me?"

"Yes, definitely. Just let go of this painful episode, and be open to new possibilities," Logan answered.

"Do you have a new possibility, Mr. Reid?" Darren was weaving on his feet.

"Yes, her name is Zoey."

"Oh, that's so sweet." Darren began sobbing again.

A cop car pulled up. The siren and lights were turned off now, and a cop got out of the police car.

"Chito, can you please tell Darren what's going to happen now?" Logan asked.

"Darren, my officer is going to take you in and put you in a cell until you sober up."

Darren nodded. "I need to sober up. I drank too much. I guess I goofed up."

"Yes, but it could have been worse. Time to go with my officer." Chito gestured to the officer who was carrying handcuffs.

"Okay." Darren turned to the cop. Logan could hear him singing, "*Don't worry. Be happy*" as the cop took him away and put him in the backseat of the police car.

Chito turned to Logan. "Thanks for the help, but you know that could have gone bad really quickly."

"Yeah, I know. But he's a good kid, and I didn't want you to have to shoot him."

Chito nodded. "I think I'll go back to bed now."

"Me, too."

They returned together to the ground floor of Casa Pacifica. There was a woman standing in the hallway. Chito didn't know her.

"Everything's okay," Logan said. "We can all go back to bed now, Remedios."

The woman smiled and said, "Okay, I'll do that." But instead of turning to go, she took a good look at Chito, his shirtless chest and his pajama bottoms. There were cartoon Minions making funny faces printed on the pajamas.

"Nice pajamas." She grinned.

Chito frowned. "My daughter gave these to me for my birthday."

"Okay, back to bed. See you boys tomorrow." Remedios turned and walked away.

"Have a good sleep in those pajamas, Chito. So cute!" Logan snickered.

"Shut up, Logan." Chito growled.

Logan laughed out loud as he closed his door behind him.

Chito went into his apartment and fell into bed.

* * *

Chito Alvarez opened the door of his refrigerator to see if there was anything else he could put in this large tossed salad. He'd started with lettuce, then added cherry tomatoes cut in half, then grated carrots, and chopped peppers. He found a couple of just-ripe avocados, peeled and chopped them, and added them to the salad. Then some shredded mozzarella cheese. He sighed. He didn't like to cook, but he felt an obligation to take something to the group Sunday evening potluck. No one complained about his salads. And a big salad didn't require a recipe or actual "cooking."

Suddenly, there was a loud squealing sound outside. He felt a flash of alarm course through him. He turned to peer out the window of his apartment to the side yard where his daughter Isabel and Charlie, son of the apartment manager Logan Reid, were playing together. Squeals transformed into giggles as the two almost six-year-olds chased a greyhound dog in a big circle. Charlie quickly changed directions, Isabel followed, and now the dog, Gwenny, that was her name, was chasing the two kids.

Chito sighed. Relax, he told himself. They're just being noisy kids, having fun. Being a Tucson cop for the past twelve years meant that every time he heard a sudden noise, Chito would feel that same burst of alarm. He needed to learn to relax or he was going to end up with some stress-related health problem. "Shit," he muttered to himself. He thought about that song that Logan had sung really early this morning. Chito wondered if he'd ever stop worrying and be happy. His job came with built-in stress.

And his daughter. He loved Isabel more than he thought possible. Above all, he wanted her to be safe, and at the same time, he didn't want to smother her. She need some space to play with Charlie and Gwenny, and making squealing sounds was part of her play. Isabel was having fun, and that's good, he told himself. Let her be.

Chito turned back to the salad, decided he was done, so he slid it onto a refrigerator shelf. He shook his head and frowned. He'd done more food prep since he moved into Casa Pacifica Apartments than he'd ever done in his life. Most of the time, he just stopped off at a local restaurant for carry-out, or maybe went by a food truck and got a quick meal. He frequently ate at his desk in his office at Tucson Police Department headquarters, or he ate at home alone. Since Isabel spent all week with her mom and her step-dad and half-siblings, he only had to provide meals for her on the weekends. And sometimes not even then.

But now, everything had changed. Every Sunday evening, he joined the other residents of Casa Pacifica Apartments to eat together and to have a good time at the weekly potluck dinner. He was surprised at how much he really enjoyed these group potlucks. The residents were all very amiable and supportive of his work. But he didn't really enjoy messing with the food prep. He was going to have to think about that. Either really learn how to cook and enjoy it, or start buying something to bring to the potlucks. But what? He looked at the clock. Residents would meet at Logan and Zoey's apartment for the potluck in a couple of hours.

Suddenly, another loud sound interrupted his thoughts, but this time it wasn't a squeal but more of a scream. Again, that instant burst of alarm went through him. Chito looked out and saw Isabel sitting on the ground crying. He quickly turned and ran from his apartment, slamming the door behind him, and he arrived at Isabel's side in less than ten seconds. Isabel was sobbing now.

"What happened?" Chito asked, kneeling next to Isabel.

Charlie spoke first. "Isabel fell. She skidded on the gravel over there and landed her knees." Chito looked at Charlie and nodded. He could see that Charlie had a very distressed look on his face.

Chito could see that there were scrapes on both of Isabel's knees, but one knee was especially injured. Blood was dripping down her leg, and Chito could see bits of dirt and pebbles in the wound.

"It hurts, Daddy." Isabel sobbed again.

Gwenny came forward and tried to lick Isabel's face.

"Charlie, hold on to Gweeny. I have to take Isabel inside," Chito said.

"Can I help?"

The sound of a woman's voice startled Chito. He looked up. She was very close to him, and he hadn't even noticed her. Too focused on Isabel. "She scraped her knees. I'm taking her in."

Chito realized that the woman was the same one he'd seen really early that morning, the one who had complimented his cartoon pajama bottoms. Remedios. Yeah, that was her name.

The woman knelt down next to them. She spoke directly to Isabel in a soft, comforting voice, a smile on her face. "What's your name, sweetie?"

"Isabel." She pointed to her knee. "It hurts."

"Let me take a closer look." The woman knelt down next to Isabel. She was facing Chito now. "I think we can fix this, Isabel."

Chito frowned. Okay, she was trying to be nice, but she was being sort of intrusive. Who the hell was she? He didn't really know her. And where had she come from? "You don't have to do this. I'll take care of her," he said firmly.

The woman looked at Chito and smiled. "I'm sure you can take care of her. But I'm a nurse practitioner, and I have several years' experience working in my hospital's emergency room. Taking care of Isabel and people like her is what I do."

"Oh," Chito said, surprised. A nurse practitioner was up the hierarchy from a regular registered nurse, closer to a doctor. And with emergency room experience. "Okay. What should we do? And who are you?"

"I'm Remedios Davila. Remember me from early this morning? You live here, right?"

"Yes. I remember you. I'm Chito Alvarez, and this is my daughter Isabel."

"And I'm Charlie. Isabel is my friend," Charlie added.

Remedios smiled again. "I suggest you take Isabel to your apartment. I'll join you in a minute with supplies." She stood and walked back up the front stairs and into Casa Pacifica Apartments, disappearing quickly.

Chito picked up Isabel and cradled her in his arms. "Come on, Charlie. Let's go in. Bring Gwenny. But you'll have to make her sit and behave."

"I will. I promise," Charlie said.

Two minutes later, they were back in Chito's apartment. He'd just placed Isabel on a chair when there was a knock on his door. "Charlie, go open the door for me, please." Charlie complied.

Remedios Davila entered the apartment with a smile on her face. She was carrying a leather bag, similar to what Chito thought of as a doctor's medical bag. She pulled up a chair and sat facing Isabel.

"Here's what we're going to do. First, I'm going to put to sleep the hurt in your knee. Your daddy is going to put a towel over your face while you are holding your breath. Do you know how to hold your breath?"

So calm. So professional. Chito was grateful that Remedios had appeared.

"Yes, I know how to hold my breath," Isabel said, her voice trembling.

"Chito, do you have a little towel?"

He stood and found a clean, folded dish towel in his kitchen.

Remedios pulled a spray bottle of topical anesthetic from her bag. "When I say 'go,' we're all going to hold our breath. And your daddy is going to put the towel over your face."

"Me, too? Can I hold my breath, too?" Charlie asked. He giggled.

"Yes. All of us. Not the dog, though." Remedios looked at Chito and wiggled her eyebrows. "You, too, Chito."

Chito smiled. Calm, professional, and charming, too.

"Ready?" Everyone nodded.

"Okay. One...Two...Three. Go!"

All four of them took a deep breath and held it. Chito quickly placed the towel over his daughter's face just as Remedios sprayed the topical anesthetic onto her injured knee. She turned and made a gesture to Chito to remove the towel.

"Great! We can breathe again!"

"It doesn't hurt anymore," Isabel said, surprise in her voice.

"Not for a while. It will hurt again, and then it will hurt less, and then less, and then it will stop hurting altogether. I'm going to clean your wound now, and put an antibiotic cream on it." Remedios proceeded to do just that.

Chito watched. Finally he said, "What do you think about the wound? What should I do?"

"It's painful but not really a deep wound, just a nasty scrape. You'll need to watch it and make sure that no signs of infection appear."

"Okay. I'll tell her mother. She and I are divorced, and I only have Isabel on the weekends."

"Tell her mom to watch for any pain, inflammation, redness, or swelling, which is an early sign of infection. I'll give you some antibiotic cream to give to her."

Chito nodded. "I'll follow your instructions."

Remedios stood. "It was nice meeting you all."

Chito stood. "I don't know how to thank you."

"My pleasure. Like I said, this is what I do." She smiled again, turned, and headed toward the door.

"Wait. Please," Chito said. He wanted to know more about her. "Are you staying here?"

"Yes, I quit my job at the hospital where I worked in Texas, and I've returned to Tucson to live. I'm looking for a new job now. I'm staying with my sister, Frida."

"Frida?" Chito was surprised. Remedios was nothing like Frida, the union strike leader who was something of a hell raiser, and who had been arrested five times.

"Yes, Frida. She's my big sister. Half-sister really, because we have different dads. I'm staying with her until I find a new job and an apartment of my own."

"Oh," Chito said, at a loss for words now. Remedios was nothing, nothing, nothing like Frida. She was calm and competent and reassuring...and very pretty. Dark, shoulder-length hair, big brown eyes, a dimple in one cheek when she smiled. Lovely. He blurted out, "You're not like Frida."

Remedios laughed. "No. We're different for sure. But we get along well." By this time, she was half-way out the door. She turned back and said, "So I'll see you at the potluck?"

"Oh, yeah, the potluck. We'll be there."

Remedios waved at everyone and left Chito's apartment, closing the door behind her.

Chito turned to the two children. "Okay, Isabel. Looks like you are in better shape now. How about if we find something for you two to do that is a little calmer?"

"Can we watch TV?" Charlie asked. "My daddy lets me watch TV sometimes."

Chito smiled. He knew from talking to Logan that Charlie's access to the television was restricted, and he wasn't allowed to have any digital devices at all. Logan had opinions about that sort of thing.

"Okay. You can watch the PBS Kids channel." Chito turned on the TV.

"Yippie!" Charlie said. "*Nature Cat* is coming on now. I love *Nature Cat*."

"I love *Nature Cat*, too." Isabel sat down on the sofa in front of the television. Charlie and Gwenny joined them on the sofa.

Chito sighed with relief as the two children became caught up in *Nature Cat*'s story. He could see that the animated cartoon story featured a big yellow cat with a purple nose that became a backyard explorer as soon as his humans left home for work everyday. Logan would approve.

After about twenty minutes of *Nature Cat*, Chito heard a soft knock at his door. He opened the door and found Logan Reid standing there.

"Hey, Logan. Come on in."

"No, thanks. I'm just here for a minute. We just got back from the market. Is it okay for Charlie to stay with you until it's time for you to come to our place? Zoey and I need to make something for us to contribute to the potluck."

"Sure. They were playing outside with the dog, and now they're watching the PBS Kids' channel."

"Has Charlie been good?"

"Very good. He and Isabel get along great."

"Okay. Then we'll see you at the potluck." Logan turned to go.

* * *

Chito managed to carry his large salad bowl and a couple of bottles of salad dressing safely to the potluck, all while herding two rambunctious kids and a big dog in front of him. Lucky for him, Logan and Zoey's apartment door was just a few feet away. Logan directed Chito to put the salad on the long dinner table, already set with dinner plates, wine glasses, and several other dishes.

He put his salad bowl with the other dishes, then looked around the room. Zoey, Logan's wife, was in the kitchen stirring something on the stove. Seated around the room were other Casa Pacifica residents: veterinarian Angela and photographer Marc who lived together upstairs; artist Xochi and chef Li who also lived upstairs. Chito knew Xochi and Li were a couple, but he wasn't sure who lived where. Frida, the other downstairs resident, wasn't present. But Remedios Davila was there. Remedios, Frida's half sister; Remedios, the nurse practitioner who had treated his daughter with loving kindness; Remedios with the one dimple. She smiled and waved at him. Chito returned her smile. He felt himself getting warm.

The dinner was just as Chito had come to expect. Good food and plenty of it. Lots of joking and laughter. He was glad he lived here. For the moment, he could forget about his work, despite what had happened early this morning. The days with his daughter Isabel and these potluck dinners were a real stress relief, often with moments of real happiness.

The meal finished, dishes were cleared away and were being washed. Logan was with the children in Charlie's bedroom. Chito could hear the kids giggling and enthusiastically demanding to see another *Nature Cat* episode, and after a moment's pause, Logan agreed. He soon returned to the adults, and everyone gathered together in front of the living room's big window, all sitting on the sofa or stuffed chairs nearby.

Logan spoke first. "I don't have much to tell. My classes at the community college are going well, mainly because I have a good group of students this semester. It's early November, and Charlie's birthday is coming up. Zoey and I are talking about how to celebrate it. He's going to be six. That's a big deal, so we want to make the birthday special. How about you, Zoey?" He reached out and took her hand.

"At the end of this semester, I'm going on leave from my teaching job at the high school," Zoey said. "And …" She stood up and thrust her stomach and belly out so that her state of pregnancy was obvious. "…I'm getting bigger by the minute. As I told you last week, Logan did a number on me, and now I'm carrying twins!" She laughed.

"I did a number on you?" Logan's eyebrows went up and a smile grew on his face. Everyone laughed.

"Boys or girls or one of each?" Angela asked.

"The doctor thinks one is a boy, but she's not sure about the other baby." Zoey sat down. "I'm happy." She turned to Angela. "What have you been up to?"

"Things are going well at the veterinary clinic. This week we managed to save a family dog that had been run over. But, unfortunately, he has only three legs now. And we took in a female Golden Retriever in the last stage of pregnancy. She gave birth and now has twelve pups."

"Whoa. That's a lot," Xochi said.

"And how can she feed so many?" Li asked.

"It is a lot," Angela said. "We're helping her with the feedings." She turned to Marc and smiled.

"I'm getting work ready for an exhibit that will be held in a big art photography gallery in Phoenix. That will be after Christmas. And I'm doing some volunteer work for an animal rescue organization that Angela told me about. I take photos of the animals, mostly dogs and cats, that show their big, sad eyes. The idea is to make them look lovable and sweet and lonely so they will be adopted."

"You're the sweet one, Marco, my love," Angela said. She kissed him.

Logan spoke now. "Frida is off organizing some grocery workers. I think she said she's out in California. You've all met Remedios, Frida's sister?" Everyone nodded.

"Hi, everyone. I'm busy looking for a job now," Remedios said.

"Am I the only one here that sees the connection between Frida and Remedios?" Xochi said. She looked around the room.

"They're sisters," Logan answered.

Xochi made a face. "Anyone ever take an art history class?" she asked impatiently.

Chito noticed that Remedios was grinning. "I always wondered if Frida was named after Frida Kahlo, that famous Mexican artist," he said.

"Exactly. Very good, Chito," Xochi said. "And Remedios?"

No one said anything.

"Oh, you are all hopeless. Remedios Varo!"

"Tell us about Remedios Varo," Zoey said.

"She was a Spanish artist who left Spain, went to France, and then she fled France when the Nazis took over. She ended up in Mexico and lived there the rest of her life. She was a surrealist painter."

Remedios was nodding her head again and grinning.

"Okay, so none of us knows much about art history. Sorry about that, Xochi," Logan smiled. "I understand that you and Li have a big announcement."

Xochi and Li jumped up, holding hands and grinning.

"You already know about Li and his food truck gig. That's going really great! And here's what's new. We're opening an art gallery and a music venue!" Xochi said. Her voice was full of excitement.

"That's right," Li added. He was grinning and sounded just as excited as Xochi. "We bought that old laundromat next to the market a few blocks from here."

"We had enough money to do that because we sold that Chinese scroll and several other antique books my grandfather left me," Xochi added.

Li continued, "That gave us the money both to buy the building and remodel it. We've been working on the upgrades since the summer."

"The big front room will be the art gallery." Xochi grinned.

"We'll get to see Xochi's work and sometimes other artists," Li added.

"The back room will be my studio. And there's a bathroom, too." Xochi grinned.

"And Xochi can teach classes there. We hired workers to put in a skylight," Li said.

"The gallery will also be a venue for musical events. Solo artists and small groups. Li will be first. He'll play his guitar." Xochi looked up at Li and patted his cheek.

"Yeah." Li looked embarrassed. "Xochi thinks my jazz guitar isn't too bad."

"You're very good!" Xochi put her arms around Li. "Don't forget that!"

147

Li leaned down and kissed her. "You are very good, too." He wiggled his eyebrows.

"Oh, stop it!" Xochi collapsed into giggles.

"So, who is coming to our opening next Saturday evening?" Li looked around the room.

Logan, Zoey, Angela, and Marc all raised their hands.

"Sounds like a fun date with my man," Zoey said. Logan took her hand and kissed it.

"How about you, Chito?" Li asked. "You can bring a date."

Chito suddenly had a look of dismay on his face. He shook his head. "I'm boring. I work all the time. I don't know any women."

Remedios grinned and said, "Yes, you do. You know me." She stood up. "Chito Alvarez, will you be my date for the opening?"

Chito gasped. "Me? You want me to go with you?"

Everyone laughed.

"Duh," Angela said. She elbowed Chito. "Say yes."

"Uh. Well. Uh. Okay. If you don't mind." Chito looked at Remedios.

She chuckled. "I don't mind. I'll come to your place to pick you up, and we'll walk together to the opening."

Xochi and Li went back to describing all the plans that they had for their new art gallery and music venue. Questions were asked, and answers came quickly and enthusiastically.

Chito sat quietly, not really knowing what to say. It had been a long time since he'd been on a date. A really long time. He suddenly remembered what time it was right now.

"Sorry, folks. I have to take Isabel home now. She has school tomorrow."

Chito called for Isabel, and as they left Logan and Zoey's apartment, everyone waved goodbye.

About the Author

C.J. Shane is an artist and writer based in Tucson, Arizona, USA. She is the author of the Letty Valdez mystery series, the Cat Miranda mystery series, and the Iron Horse mystery series.